BELOVED VIKING

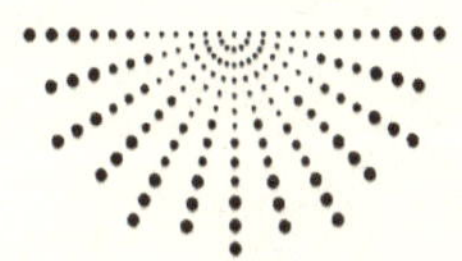

REE THORNTON

Till min vikingaman och mina två vikingabarn.

ACKNOWLEDGMENTS

This book is for my husband, who graciously shares me with the seemingly endless hours of writing, writer's group meetings, and retreats. None of this would have been possible without your support and love.

To my family and friends, of which there are far too many to name (you know who you are), thank you for always believing in me and pushing me to chase my dreams.

A special thank you to my Writers not Waiters girls, Elsa Holland, Josie Baker, Sara Hartland, L.J. Langdon, and Dana Mitchell for the unwavering support. I am truly blessed to have such wonderful friends.

Much gratitude and love to the awesome Rachel Bailey for all of the sage advice, encouragement, and for challenging me to become a better writer. I have no doubt that fate brought you into my life to guide me on this journey, and I am thankful every day that I have such a kind, generous friend in my life.

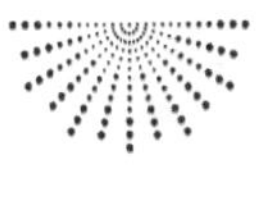

CHAPTER ONE

RÚNA

Rúna stood in the shadow of a central pillar, watching her four suitors on the far side of the great hall. The soft tones of a flute filled the room as she trailed her fingers across the tales of the All Father, Óðinn, carved into the wood.

"Damn Ràsmus Eriksson to Hel," she muttered under her breath.

Somehow, the Jarl who controlled the isle of Gottland had heard of her plan to choose a husband from one of the powerful clans and had sent a son to vie for her hand. The unexpected arrival of the added suitor and his twenty warriors had caused uproar as the whole clan scrambled to clean another barn to lodge the uninvited guests.

Her stomach rumbled at the delicious aromas of the succulent meat on the air. Now she was tired, hungry, and late to greet the men she had chosen to vie for her hand in marriage.

How could Ràsmus Eriksson think she would marry one of his sons after what had happened last time?

She sighed.

Memories of Jorvan had flooded her senses at the sight of the dragonship cutting across the bay with its sail flying at half-mast below the billowing dark blue Eriksson flag. Even now, she ached for the taste of his lips, and the tender touch that had awakened her to the pleasures between a man and woman.

"Which one is the Eriksson?" Ásta whispered in her ear.

She whirled around. "Ásta, do not sneak up on me like that."

"So which one is he?"

"I do not know." Rúna studied the table of her suitors, unable to see anything of the faces hidden behind the masks they wore from this distance.

Ásta followed her gaze across the room. "It would help if your father did not insist they wear masks. A happy match needs both an alliance and attraction."

Rúna shrugged. "An alliance is all that matters." Her father was getting older, and as his body weakened so too would his position as Jarl. She clenched her jaw and firmed her resolve. She needed to wed to ensure the succession passed to her. "I need a husband, preferably one from a family with a large army of warriors that will quell any thoughts of treachery from the other clans."

Ásta crossed her arms and huffed, the unconscious action betraying that her friend was not the handmaiden she claimed to be. "It is cruel to prevent you from seeing your husband's face until you have wed."

"Já," Rúna agreed. "I do not like it. Choosing from masked suitors is not ideal. There is much you can tell from looking upon a man's face—a little tick under his eye when lying or a twitch around his mouth when angry..."

She wanted to see the face of the man that would rule at her side, but her father was Jarl and his word was law.

"… but it is a battle not worth fighting."

"Rúna—"

"Nei, Ásta." She held up her hand to silence her friend. "This is how it must be. It will be struggle enough to take a husband—at least this way the decision is mine."

Ásta threw her a sympathetic look and nodded. Rúna knew that her friend understood well the suffering that followed losing control of your fate. It was exactly what had led Ásta to Luleavst three years ago.

Rúna shook off her self-pitying thoughts. Five summers had passed since Jorvan had broken their betrothal and abandoned her to go raiding. He had never returned. Ràn, goddess of the seas, had claimed him. It was time to let him go.

"I will choose one of these men, but the thought of marrying one of his brothers and living with the constant reminder of his ghost makes me ill. I cannot do it. I will not."

Ásta place a comforting hand on her shoulder and squeezed. "You deserve to be happy, Rúna. The Eriksson son cannot be turned away, so you must choose another."

Ásta spoke true. Rasmus Erikson was an important trading partner—it would provoke war to shun his son.

"If I can discover which mask the son wears, then I can choose another without causing offence."

She looked at the men across the room. She dismissed the one wearing the bright colours of the Sámi northerners, and another was far too tall. She studied the broad shoulders of the two remaining men. One stood to the side, watching the others laugh and drink. His relaxed bearing was that of a man who knew he belonged and felt no need to prove it.

Her breath quickened. He stood with the same confidence as Jorvan. "That one has the same golden hair as Jorvan," she mused.

Her heart ached at the memory of his hair trailing across her skin, his hands gripping her tight as he had rocked them into oblivion. As three moons had waxed and waned, they had stolen every moment they could to be together. Hiking in the woods, lazing in the meadow, kissing behind the barn, and then she'd surrendered her innocence to him willingly, laying her heart and soul bare. She'd loved him with all of her being. It had been a terrible mistake.

"I know that look, Rúna. It was not your fault he left."

She forced her expression back to the controlled mask of a shield-maiden. "Yet I was the foolish girl who thought he loved me."

Jorvan had swatted her pleas away like a fly when she'd begged him to take her with him, and then sailed away without looking back. He had broken her, and it was her own fault.

"You were young. There is no fault in seeking love. You may come to love another."

Rúna shook her head vehemently. "Love is not for me. The day he left, I vowed never to let a man or love have such power over me again. It is why I am a shield-maiden. I'd rather die than break that promise to myself."

Ásta placed a comforting hand on her shoulder. "Your vow saved my life, and for that I am glad. Yet, it saddens me that you will not know a love like I had with Njal, but I understand why you made this choice. I too would rather join the gods than cede my life to a treacherous man." The auburn hair that fell in waves around her pale face gave Ásta the look of an otherworldly seer as she spoke with a maturity well beyond her years, and then turned to resume her duties and serve ale to the revellers.

Rúna sighed. She wished she could do something to ease her friend's suffering, wished she could offer more than shelter and protection.

Frode, the boat builder's hound, collided with her leg, snapping her out of her musings and back to the problem at hand. She watched as he scampered past and disappeared under a table on the hunt for discarded scraps and bones, her gaze drifting to the man standing separate from the other suitors sitting and drinking at the table.

A disguising mask and shadows obscured his face. Was he the Eriksson son?

As though sensing he was being watched, he looked over his shoulder.

She froze as a rush of awareness made the hair on her arms stand on end, as, for a few heart-pounding moments, he searched the shadows where she stood.

Could he see her? Was he as reluctant to be here as she was to have him as a suitor?

Her shoulders sagged and her hand fell from the engraved pillar when he turned away and returned to watching the crowd.

She squared her shoulders and stepped forward. It was time to choose a husband.

CHAPTER TWO

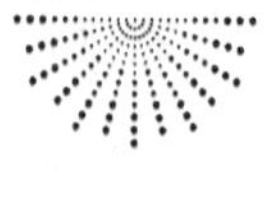

JORVAN

*J*orvan leaned against the rough timber wall and feasted on the sight of the woman he loved hiding behind a pillar. He had been foolish to leave her five years ago, swayed by his battered pride and foolish notions of adventure and gold. It was yet another failure to add to the dark turbulent sea of regret that threatened to pull him under. Now he was back at Luleavst and determined not to make the same mistake again.

A hand clasped his shoulder and squeezed. "Are you certain this is what you want, brother?"

His skin crawled beneath the gentle touch, and then a shiver crept down his spine. He had become deft at hiding the weakness, but nowadays a simple touch was a difficult burden to bear. He shook the hand from his shoulder. How had he forgotten that Valen treated all eight of his younger siblings as if they were his children?

He met his brother's concerned gaze with one of steadfast resolve. "I think of little else."

Valen sighed and shook his head. "Rúna will not forgive you easily."

He knew Valen was voicing his concern in the hopes of saving him the misery of inevitable rejection, but he'd not let anyone divert him from this course.

"I deserve her wrath. It was a mistake to leave her."

"Rúna is the least of your worries. The Jarl is coming over," Valen said out of the corner of his mouth.

Jorvan watched the first hurdle in his quest to win Rúna back storm across the crowded room. Jarl Karl Isaksson's hair had lightened to the gray of an old man and there were more lines around his eyes, but his thin lips were still twisted into the same distasteful scowl as when they had last met—when he had been caught sneaking back from the meadow where he'd made love to Rúna. The Jarl had suspected treachery was afoot and accused him of plotting against clan Isaksson.

Jorvan steeled himself for the battle ahead. Clearly, the uneasy peace that had been negotiated between his father and Karl Isaksson during his absence had disappeared now that he had returned. In truth, he had not forgiven the man who had driven him away from the woman he loved and into the depths of Hel, either.

Jarl Isaksson had laughed at his request to marry his daughter. *You will never be good enough for the likes of my Rúna, traitor.*

Jarl Isaksson's words had hit him like a fist to the gut. Her father was right—she was kind and pure, and he had been a drunk without lands or wealth. He'd had nothing to offer her.

If you truly love her, you will leave and let her make a good marriage.

And so he'd left. He had rounded up his warriors and the

few Isaksson men he'd befriended over ale, and caught on a tide of reckless abandon and a foolish notion to seek his fortune, he'd gone raiding. It was only many moons later, while held captive, that he'd finally admitted to himself that he'd used the Jarl's words as an excuse to leave her behind because he'd felt unworthy.

"Jarl Isaksson." Jorvan nodded respectfully at the glowering man who halted in front of him, noticing that his once strong body had begun to wither.

"Why are you here?" Karl Isaksson hid none of his dislike under a pleasant tone.

Jorvan crossed his arms and met the Jarl's furious gaze with one of steely determination.

"You know why."

He'd never cede to this man again. Losing his brothers at arms had taught him a powerful lesson. Life was short. He'd fight until his last breath to honor the memory of his comrades and win back the woman he loved. And he did love Rúna, of that he was certain. It was the memories of their love, and the desire to hold her in his arms again, that had kept him alive.

"Then it is best you leave," the Jarl scoffed.

Jorvan narrowed his eyes and stood his ground. Karl Isaksson would not win this time. "I am here to stay."

The Jarl's nostrils flared and he skimmed his calculating gaze downward, taking in Jorvan's muscular body, strengthened by relentless training during the long journey home, and then his eyes flicked upward once more.

Jorvan met his stony glare, allowing the man to see a flicker of the darkness that lurked within him.

The Jarl's gaze became wary.

Good. He had no desire to war with the man. Rúna would never forgive him for killing her father.

"What happened to you?" the Jarl demanded.

He crossed his arms slowly, enjoying making the Jarl wait. "Did you not hear I died?"

The Jarl's jaw tensed at his mocking tone. "What of my drunkard men that went raiding with you?"

Remorse filled Jorvan at the mention of his men and the question he'd been dreading. The Jarl's lingering animosity was warranted. Rúna's father was still bitter that his men had chosen to go raiding with a man that he considered a traitor, and he had not even learned of their fate yet.

Jorvan ground his teeth. He was responsible for their deaths and no apology would ever suffice. There was no way to soften the blow of such a loss. "Do not insult the dead or you shall feel the bite of my sword. They were good men, and honorable to the end."

Jarl Isaksson rocked back on his heels and studied him curiously. "They are dead? What happened to you?" His tone was softer, but just as demanding.

"They died. I lived," Jorvan replied with a steely thread of warning in his voice, and then pressed his lips together. In time, he would request an audience with the Jarl to offer an explanation and his condolences, but he'd give no further answers in this crowded room. He would not let the fate of his men be fodder for gossip.

The Jarl glanced across the room.

Jorvan followed his gaze.

Firelight flickered across Rúna's flaxen hair as she crossed the room, the hem of her simple blue dress floating grace-fully across the floor as she moved with the urgency of a woman with purpose. Her slender waist and hips now dipped and curved in the sensual figure of a woman, and her unbound hair fell down around her shoulders save for the few braids at the front that framed her angular face and high cheekbones.

His heart thundered in his chest. Óðinn, she was an stunning.

The Jarl threw him a look of disgust. "She'll never welcome you, since you abandoned her afore," he said. Then abandoning any pretence of civility, he turned and strode back to where his wife sat on the raised dais.

Valen, who had remained silent throughout the entire exchange, finally spoke. "Do you think that truth? Is this an impossible task?"

"Mayhap…" He could feel his brother's concerned stare like a rash spreading across his skin. He was weary of fending off the pitiful looks of his family. They treated him as though he were a cripple, as if he'd returned a lesser man because he cringed from their touch, and was haunted by nightmares and the darkness that reminded him of his cavernous prison. Curse them! He'd rather they treat him as if he were still dead. At least there would be honor in that.

"I will marry her." He just had to convince her now.

"If that is what you want, then I support you, brother."

"It is." Any doubt disappeared the moment Rúna had stepped into the great hall and he'd felt the invisible pull between them. At least that hadn't changed.

She was even more beautiful than he remembered. His cock swelled as he devoured her with his eyes. Something was different about her. What was it? He tracked her move-ment across the room as he waved off the handmaiden attempting to refill his untouched cup of ale.

Rúna paused beside a table of Isaksson warriors devouring chunks of venison.

Was one of them her lover?

His grip tightened around the carved wooden cup. He must discover if one of the Isaksson warriors had claimed her heart in his absence. He memorized each of their faces as they met her gaze with nods. Why did they not stand and greet her properly?

The one nearest her, an older dark-haired man with a flattened nose, placed a double-edged sword on the table and spoke.

Rúna reached out and trailed her hand over the smooth surface as she replied.

Jorvan's breath caught. It was dangerous to touch such a sharp weapon.

She lifted the sword from the table, and then cut through the air with swift precision, her stance wide and centered, the muscles in her arm flexing as she moved the heavy weapon with ease. She laid it back on the table and nodded her approval.

When had she learnt to wield a sword? Heaviness settled in his stomach.

Shield-maiden!

Rúna wasn't just their comrade. The man had sought her approval—she was their leader! She must have seen many battles for the Isaksson warriors to afford her such respect. How had the gentle girl he'd known become a shield-maiden?

His stomach churned at the thought of her surrounded by the blood and gore of war. No wonder she seemed different—war changed a person. The girl he'd known would be long gone. He lowered his cup to hide the stiff outline of his cock pushing against his breeches. Blessed Freya, that she was a fierce warrior impressed him and made him want her even more. How did one win over a battle-hardened shield-maiden?

Suddenly, the gentle caress of the flute that had swirled around the lively room all eve disappeared.

He froze at the distinctive thump of hands hitting a magic drum.

Three young girls weaved through the tables, their distinctive blood red gowns of seers-in-training giving the illusion that they were floating. Their hands beat in flawless rhythm as they moved toward where Jarl Isaksson sat at the center of the hall.

Seiðkonur!

Panic tore at his insides as the clawing hands of the past wrapped around his throat and squeezed. He struggled for air, his every nerve ending aflame with the warning that preceded danger.

A blast of icy air gusted through the open door, as though blown in by the frost giants of Jǫtunheimr.

Jorvan shivered. It wasn't even winter yet. *Was this one of Loki's tricks?* His hand fell to the hilt of his sword as a hooded figure loomed in the doorway.

The noisy din vanished as he watched the dark cloak fall to the floor, revealing the slender figure of a woman gripping the long carved magic staff of a seiðkonur. Sacred runic symbols covered the length of her arms, and the black kohl lines that a seer wore during ceremony crossed her pale face.

Bile rose in his throat, accompanied by the overwhelming urge to flee.

Stealthy darkness wrapped its fetid coils around his heart as the taste of the rancid brew the seiðkonur had fed him filled his mouth. He'd cursed the evil witch every time she'd forced the concoction that made him cooperate down his throat, but resistance was futile with his hands and feet bound to the sacred altar.

Night after night, the vile witch had laughed at his

distress as she'd rubbed the oils into his body and then performed the bloodletting ritual, seeking the favor of the gods in her quest to repopulate her dying clan with new children.

His stomach heaved at the memory. He'd been fortunate that she'd wanted to keep him alive, though sometimes when the tortured screams of his men dying haunted him at night he had wished he were dead. He clenched his jaw and willed his heartbeat back to a smooth hollow thump.

The evil witch was dead.

He'd watched her die.

The seiðkonur crossed the room, her long silver hair dancing like spellbinding flames, her beady gaze challenging the revellers until their hushed whispers fell to utter silence. As she passed by, she paused in front of each of the masked suitors, her eyes scanning them as though assessing their worth.

His chest was so tight he couldn't breathe.

It's not her. It's not her.

Every muscle in his body was taut, prepared to pounce and cut down the murderous witch she had become in his mind.

Did the seer know what had happened to him? Is that what she had seen in her visions? Will she whisper unfavorably in the Jarl's ear of his torment and weakness?

The seiðkonur waved her hand and the drumming quieted to a dull drone, like a heart beating in the background.

"Jarl Isaksson," she said as she stopped before him.

Her soft voice snapped Jorvan back to reality. This was not the hoarse throaty tone of his tormentor.

"Well met, Seda." Jarl Isaksson nodded in greeting. "Do you come to join the feast?"

"Nei. The gods have spoken."

Jorvan clenched his teeth. Many clans had a seiðkonur that offered prophecies, but Rúna's father had long had an unnatural trust of his seer. The fool did not know the depths of evil that could dwell in the hearts of those that claimed connection with the other worlds, those that would do anything to gain favor with the gods.

Jarl Isaksson leaned forward in his chair, his gaze intent on the woman. "What say the gods? Have they spoken of my daughter's marriage?"

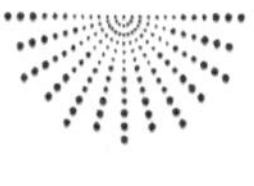

CHAPTER THREE

RÚNA

Rúna rolled her eyes and waited for the seer to speak. Although Seda was much older than the Jarl, it seemed as though she defied time. Her father often visited Seda at her hut deep in the forest, but the woman and her visions had always made Rúna wary. Though she knew Seda meant well, it sometimes felt as if the seer's piercing gray eyes were trying to steal her soul.

"Já. The gods have gifted a prophecy." Seda stood tall, her body swaying back and forth gently. "The seed of thy loins shall wed one of brawn, wit, and heart."

Rúna scoffed. There was no great revelation in her words. Seda only ever told the Jarl what he wanted to hear. Why did the gods not tell the seer something useful, such as who was stealing the combs and other items that had vanished this last moon? A shiver of foreboding crept up Rúna's spine as she watched her father caress his beard thoughtfully.

"To claim her hand he shall overcome trials in a challenge of games."

Rúna clenched her jaw. Now the seiðkonur went too far.

She already had a plan, and it was a good one. She would meet with each of the suitors, ask them questions to get to know them, and then make her decision. The last thing she wanted was the seer interfering, or her father setting even more frustrating rules intended to favor one man over another. She hurried past the sunken stone hearth toward the raised Jarl's chair. She had to put a stop to this.

"Father?"

"Tst, Daughter." He nodded at the seer. "Aye, Seda. The gods are wise. My daughter is worthy of such a challenge for her hand."

Rúna glared at Seda. How dare the seer offer her up like a prize? She was no meek woman, content to allow men to decide her fate. She was warrior, soon to be Jarl, and Seda had best learn that she would not offer the clan seer the same favor her father did.

Seda held her gaze.

"The gods have spoken, the suitors will be challenged," her father announced to the watchful crowd.

"Nei, Father. You promised I would choose. Hide their faces as we agreed. Let me ask them questions to know them better." She had to convince him, there was too much at stake. She must choose who would help her lead clan Isaksson—this was too important to be decided by Viking games.

Her father cast her a pitying look and shook his head. "The first of four trials shall begin at first light. Rúna, you may ask your questions and award the one with the most satisfying answers as victorious in that challenge."

She bit down on her tongue to hide her disappointment at his betrayal. All these years he'd assured her that she would choose her husband, and then one word from the crazy seiðkonur and he broke his word. She pressed her lips into a hard line and prepared to fight back. She'd seen the despair caused by an unhappy marriage in Helga, her childhood playmate. The woman was barely a shadow of her former self after five summers married to a man that Seda had declared the gods had chosen for her.

"I demand the right to compete. If I win I shall choose the man I wed," she said. She'd rather dwell with Loki's daughter in Hel than with a man not of her choosing.

Her father growled at her and slammed his hand down on the table in front of him. "You are a thorn in my ass, Daughter." He gave her a look she knew well, a warning to push no further lest his temper erupt.

She lowered her gaze as she spoke. "A thorn with a sword equal to any man."

He sat back in his chair, the tension easing from his shoulders at her respectful pose. "Já. You have fought honorably for our clan. You may compete."

Rúna nodded in satisfaction. She would learn about each of her suitors while she bested them, so that she could find the one who would make the best husband.

Her father rose from his chair and faced the table of masked men. "Well met, warriors. I have but one rule: lay hands on her before a wedding and you shall meet my sword."

Rúna shook her head at her father's words. He sought to protect her from the desires of men, but she was no innocent.

"Now you will greet my daughter and reveal your face."

Good. She wanted to look upon them. She turned to face the suitors as they moved forward, their faces hidden behind animal masks that left just their eyes, lips, and jaws visible.

Her heart jumped to her throat at the sight of the man she'd watched earlier.

The soft golden fur and long muzzle of the wolf mask hid his face, but ice blue eyes surrounded by a ring as dark as the skin of a blueberry stared back at her—Eriksson eyes.

The air around her seemed to thicken, making it difficult to draw breath.

Her pulse began to flutter, but… Nei. She couldn't do this, not with Jorvan's brother. The very thought of it left her shaken. It was merely his resemblance to Jorvan that had brought these feelings to the surface once more. She pulled her gaze from that too familiar stare and turned to face the nearest man.

"Welcome, Fox."

He wobbled sightly from too much mead, his glassy emerald gaze surrounded by the white fur and delicate features of the winter fox.

Rúna looked him up and down. The mask was all that was delicate about this mountain of a man with shoulders as wide as two men and legs like tree trunks.

"Remove your mask," her father ordered.

A large hand criss-crossed with battle scars pulled the mask from his face. "Well met, Rúna. I am Leif, brother of Jarl Siv Gustafsson."

"Well met, Leif." She nodded at the man and tried to avoid looking at the large bump on his nose, certain that it was the result of a bad break.

Beside him, brown feathers fanned outwards from the hooked nose of an eagle mask, crowned by three white-tipped feathers above a pair of gray eyes.

"Eagle. I thank you for making the journey."

This man barely reached the shoulder of the towering giant beside him.

The eagle bowed his head. "W-w-well met," he stammered, before straightening his back and smiling at her.

His soft hairless jaw told her he was not quite a man, yet there was a gentle strength to his demeanor. It was unusual to see the distinctive Sámi garb this far south, and even less so to see it worn with a Viking blade, belt, and axe. Could she mold him into a good leader?

His hand shook as he pushed the mask up onto his forehead. "I am Dànel Kvitfjell, from the Sámi lands of the north."

Rúna smiled at him gently. "Well met, Dànel."

"Who is next?" her father asked impatiently.

The man in the mask with small ears topped by distinctive white tufts stepped forward.

"Welcome, Lynx." Had her father matched the masks to the men? The feline was a formidable hunter. Did the mask hide a man with those qualities?

"My thanks, Rúna. Your invitation honors my family." His voice was smooth and strong—it reminded her of the gentle purr of the grain room cats.

"As your presence honors mine."

Dark brown eyes with flecks of amber that matched the lynx's mottled fur stared back at her with intelligence. She tilted her head to the side—here was a contender.

"Take it off or we shall be here until dawn," her father said, his tone unusually gruff about the delay.

The man removed the mask, revealing a head closely shaved on both sides, with a mass of brown hair down the middle that flopped over to the left and down his forehead.

"Jàrri Karlsson of Tronðheim." He smiled, drawing her attention to his thin lips surrounded by deep red facial hair trimmed close to his face and angular jaw.

She smiled back. His clan was powerful and he was not without appeal, an interesting prospect.

Unable to avoid it any longer, Rúna turned to face the

piercing Eriksson gaze. Her heart hammered in a rhythm that matched the low drone of the drums.

"Well met, Wolf."

"Rúna," he replied, his voice a low rumble.

Her breath caught for a moment.

He was leaning against the wall, partially hidden by the shadows, his arms crossed against his chest as his hungry gaze scanned her body.

A shiver crept up her spine.

The white shirt that he wore did little to hide the narrow waist that tapered outwards into broad shoulders covered in the long golden hair that fell from his head.

She crossed her arms over her chest to resist the urge to reach out and brush it away. She could not allow this to go any further. Loki was toying with her, tricking her mind into recreating Jorvan in a desperate attempt to bring him back from the dead. She recalled what she knew of Jorvan's brothers. Arik and Halvor would still be children, and Ivvar and Rorik had flaming red hair. This must be Úlf, Erik, Valen, or Njal. Could she bring herself to spend her life with a man who reminded her of Jovan? Nei, she couldn't do it. It wouldn't be fair to either of them.

Casually, the wolf's eyes tracked her assessing gaze, then fell to her mouth and flared as she scraped her teeth across her bottom lip.

Someone tossed a log on the fire, sending up sparks and casting light on the faded line of a scar that curved from beneath his trimmed beard upward across his right cheek and disappeared beneath the mask.

Fenrisúlfr!

Rúna shivered as Loki's wolf-son flashed in her mind. Her father had chosen well—the mask matched the man behind it.

"Enough. Take it off," her father roared.

She flinched. Why was he so out of sorts this eve? He should be pleased that she would soon be wed and his legacy secured.

The wolf stepped from the shadows into the light, his hands covering his face as he reached for the mask.

Her heart raced.

His hard bulging muscles flexed as he lowered his arms.

Rúna stared into the blue eyes and familiar face of a dead man.

"Nei!"

She stumbled backward.

A strangled cry tore from her chest in one painful breath-stealing blow. "Jorvan?"

"Well met, Rúna."

Images flashed in her mind. Standing on the beach with the straps of her hastily packed bag cutting into her shoulder as he told her he'd never let a soft girl weigh him down. Frozen in shock, unable to reconcile the man she had surrendered her innocence to just a few hours earlier with the one sailing away. Then falling to her knees, breaking inside, as though the man she loved had struck her heart with his battleaxe.

How...?

"Nei," she gasped. "You're dead." She barely heard the dulled sound of her own voice breaking at the shock. Jorvan was dead. She'd mourned him, and then renewed her vow never to let a man control her heart or her fate again.

"I live yet."

Jorvan lived.

As her shock subsided, she became aware that the silence of the room was deafening. Even the drums had ceased as all watched the spectacle unfold. Her temper flared to life and then built to a raging inferno. He had abandoned her with cruel harsh words and let her think he was dead.

"All I see is the ghost of a dead man," she said, and threw him a look of utter contempt. Now he came as a suitor for her hand, as though the past was of no consequence?

Jorvan remained silent, watching her warily.

She turned to her father. "He was not invited. Send him away."

Her father pursed his lips. "I cannot. He has done no wrong."

How could he say that? Jorvan had not only betrayed her, but her whole village, leaving behind families caught between that impossible place of not knowing and mourning the men that had gone with him on that fateful day. Now, he had shocked and embarrassed her in front of her whole clan. He was still as cruel and thoughtless as the day he'd abandoned her.

"You will regret returning to Luleavst, Wolf," she said, refusing to speak his name aloud. She spun around and stormed across the room. "How dare he come back here after what he did?" she hissed beneath her breath. She lowered herself into a chair at the farthest table from the man that had left her broken-hearted. This was war. Jorvan had won the first assault, but she would win the battle.

CHAPTER FOUR

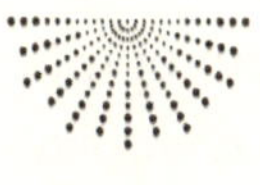

RÚNA

"Curse him to Hel for rising from the dead." Rúna stomped across the beach toward the crowd waiting for the next challenge to begin. She had wanted to drive her sword through the wolf last eve and a sleepless night had only increased her ire. He had disappeared, allowing years to pass with his friends and kin thinking him dead when he was very much alive. His selfish thoughtlessness was an unforgivable slight. Now he wanted her for a bride! How could he possibly think she'd have him after what he had done?

"Valen." She nodded at the next Eriksson Jarl. She couldn't afford to insult the man she'd need as an ally when she ruled, even though she wanted to maim his brother beside him.

"Rúna." Valen offered her a rare smile, though his eyes remained as sad and serious as ever.

She forced herself not to recoil at the pity she saw in his gaze.

"Good fortune, Brother," he said, and then hastily disappeared into the gathering crowd of spectators.

"So, how was Hel, Wolf?" She let her voice drip with the venom she felt. She knew she should be relieved that he was well, but instead she was filled with a scorching fury as she'd never felt before.

He cocked his head at her but remained silent.

Rúna studied the man she'd once loved, prepared to wait as long as it took to get an answer.

Gone was the lean youth of nineteen winters, replaced with a scarred and muscled warrior. His hair was longer, now a mass of messy golden curls that fell across his broad shoulders and bulging arms.

"Lose your tongue, Wolf?" Why did he not respond? Her gaze drifted down over the unlaced ties on the front of his shirt to the sun-kissed skin of his wide chest that tapered down to the waist where his shirt tucked into his breeches.

She bit her lip.

If she ran her hands down his stomach, she knew she'd find hard toned muscle and then the deep angular ridges that led down to his manhood. She tore her gaze away, mortified by the familiar warmth of arousal flooding her body. The primal pull to join with him was strong, but he'd used her desire against her before. Ragnarök would befall them before she'd ever let that happen again.

The wolf rubbed his short beard, drawing her attention to the puckered scar that cut across the right side of his face, which looked more like the clean deliberate slice of a dagger rather than the haphazard slice of a battle wound. He looked entirely too relaxed about waiting for her to speak again. She resisted the urge to reach out and touch it. He did not deserve her sympathy.

"You have naught to say?" She stood with her hands on her hips and gave him her deadliest glare.

He raised one bushy eyebrow. "What would you have me say?"

Rúna grit her teeth. If he offered no apology, she would give no mercy. "Why are you here?"

"You know why."

"Tell me," she demanded.

He shrugged. "I am here to win your hand."

And there he was! That all too familiar shrug of faked indifference. Finally, she recognized something about the stranger in front of her.

"I was not worthy before. I would just weigh you down, remember?"

"You have changed much," he said, as his gaze skimmed down over the curves of her body.

Heat pooled between her legs as her body betrayed her will.

"I would fall on my sword before I wed you. Get on your ship and leave."

She waited for his anger to flare. He'd always had a quick temper and she knew how to fan that fire until it blazed.

"I'm not going anywhere, firefly."

Her hands curled into fists at the calm determination in his declaration. Hearing him call her firefly again hit her in the gut like the call of the war horn signalling battle. Why wasn't he angry? It was clear that he would not back down, and his anger was no longer a weakness she could exploit.

"Don't call me that."

He tilted his head to the side and studied her. "What? Firefly?" He stepped forward, closing the distance between them. "You will always be my firefly."

"I am not your anything, *Wolf*." She pursed her lips and ignored the broad expanse of his chest. She would never be the firefly that he had claimed lit up his world—never again. He had made sure of that.

His eyes narrowed but his gaze remained unguarded, revealing both his hurt and longing.

She paused a moment, stumbling to recover from the unexpected display of emotion before firming her resolve and continuing her assault. "I'll never wed you."

His eyes darkened in an instant, pinning her in place. "We shall see."

"Even if you win, I'll not speak the words. I'd rather marry the smelly old swine farmer, Bekan." She walked off, pausing briefly to toss the final deathblow over her shoulder.

"You are still dead to me."

CHAPTER FIVE

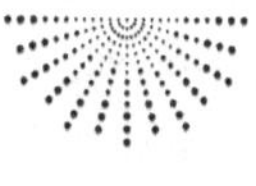

JORVAN

*L*ater that afternoon, Jorvan strode across the fallow field to the north of the village, clutching his sword.

It had been a long day of competition to eliminate the other suitors until just he and Rúna remained in this first challenge. Now, he was eager to finish this final game and claim the win that would put him in the lead.

"The axe throw was an easy victory after Leif Gustafsson threw his into that oak tree," Valen said from beside him.

"Já, but then Rúna won the archery." He glanced at where she stood talking with the Isaksson warriors, remembering how she'd glared at him after each of her arrows hit the center of the target.

"She is good with the bow," Valen said, wiping the sweat from his brow.

"Já. I taught her to shoot." An image flashed in his mind of the many days they'd spent in the meadow practicing with the bow, satisfying his need to feel her body pressed against his own.

"She has a gift for it and is a fierce opponent," Valen said with obvious admiration.

"It was a good win, but she cannot match me in this final challenge." Jorvan knew he could outlast any man at swordplay. This would not be a fair fight at all.

"I should hope not, little brother. For cert, it will be easier to best her at swordplay than win her favor."

Valen spoke true. Now that he had seen her, he knew that winning Rúna back would be much harder than he'd expected. "Her anger is warranted, but I have a plan. I shall convince her that I still love her."

Valen shook his head doubtfully. "She'll not believe you. You claimed to love her before and then you left."

"I did love her."

"I know, brother. But she will not see it like that."

"Then I shall convince her I am no longer the man that hurt her. I must show her that I have changed."

Valen shook his head and sighed. "She would forgive you faster if you tell her what happened with her father that day."

"Nei. I'll not come between her and her father."

"Then good fortune to you, Brother. You will need it," Valen said, then slapped him on the shoulder and walked off.

He watched as Rúna walked to where he waited, his gaze sweeping over her appreciatively. Every flex of her lean thighs was visible through the breeches she wore, and her sleeveless tunic did little to hide neither her womanly curves nor her well-honed muscular arms. Even all these years later, the mere sight of her stole the breath from his lungs. He almost groaned. With her hair braided back off her face, she looked every bit the courageous shield-maiden prepared for battle, and he wanted her with a fierceness that stunned him.

"Rúna," he said, nodding at her in greeting.

She turned her back on him.

He ignored her contempt. He deserved her anger, so she could goad him all she liked—he would not bite. He focused on trying to make sense of her actions. Her strong healthy body left no doubt that she trained with her clansmen, but no warrior ever exposed their back to an opponent. Did she still trust him enough to know he would not harm her? Or was she truly an untried warrior, a mere figurehead that led the Isaksson clan into battle for her father? He glanced at the sword she held in her right hand. It was smaller than his was, though just as long and sharp, but it offered no answer to her skill.

Jarl Isaksson stood beside his much smaller wife, with his arms folded across his chest. He glared at Jorvan, clearly rankled at his mere presence. "First blood wins," he declared, and nodded for the match to begin.

Rúna lifted her sword and turned.

Jorvan watched her warily, noting her bent knees and her weight centered in a fighting stance. He kept the tip of his sword to the ground. He needed to convince her of the foolishness of this game.

"We needn't do this, Rúna."

Her furious glare crushed his offer of a wise resolution. "Fight me, you coward," she said, her harsh tone brooking no argument.

He glared at the men standing at the edge of the field snickering at her insult and lifted his sword. He didn't want to do this—embarrassing her in front of her clan would just push her further away—but he couldn't see a way to avoid it.

"Get on with it," ordered her father.

Rúna leapt forward, thrusting her blade left and then right. Her eyes followed his every move as he deflected her thrusts with easy flicks of the wrist.

He bent his knees, firming his stance, and held back the

urge to smile. Her moves were solid, yet lacked force—she was testing him out and looking for weaknesses. His firefly was a wily opponent. He would play along for a while, so that she could save face before he bested her, but he would have to make it look like a real fight.

"I thought you were a shield-maiden? I've seen whelps fight harder than you."

She scowled and thrust hard for his left shoulder.

He smoothly sidestepped and whacked her blade away.

She advanced, attacking mercilessly in a dangerous dance of thrust and defence.

The cloud of dust and barley chaff kicked up by their shuffling footwork invaded his nostrils as he narrowly avoided a cunning downward thrust between his legs.

She was quick and agile, an advantage that no doubt had caught many a seasoned warrior unaware on the battlefield, but her swordplay lacked strength.

They fought until sweat ran down his chest and her breathing labored. It was time to end this, before she hurt herself in her frenzied desire to win. He lunged forward, his blade meeting hers in a series of thrusts so forceful that their blades sang as steel met steel.

Her eyes widened as she stumbled backward and fell to the dirt.

Jorvan stood above her, sword at his side, as he looked down into eyes as lush and green as a spring meadow. "Are you hurt?" When she did not answer he continued, "Do you cede?"

She flexed the fingers of her right hand as she picked up her blade with the other.

He knew the cramping pain she was feeling well. Her sword hand would ache for days. After a long battle, it was oft weeks before he could grip a weapon without flinching.

"Do you cede?" he repeated.

Her eyes darkened to the same dangerous emerald hue as the sea that swallowed ships whole, and then her left hand darted out with more speed than he'd seen her use the entire fight.

A sharp prick hit just below his knee. He blinked, and looked down at the drops of blood flowing down his leg and over the soft leather of his boot. He reeled as the dark fog descended and the bloodlust took over. He swung wildly as the witch appeared his mind, her hand covered in the blood of his men.

Kill her. Kill her.

As though through a fog, he watched Rúna scamper backward in the grass and then rise to her feet. She stood tall, her chin thrust out and her green eyes blazing with defiance. Her breathing was calm and her movements sure, as she put a hand on her hip.

Her features blurred, his beloved fading from the shield-maiden into the sneering vicious seer that had stolen his comrades and peace of mind.

"The win is mine," she said.

He barely heard her over the heavy thump of his blood pounding in his ears. She would not win. He would kill her over and over, until she haunted him no more.

Kill her. Kill her.

He roared a battle cry and attacked using all of his strength. He would send her into the icy mists of Hel where she belonged for the wrongs she had committed against her own kind.

"Cede," she commanded as she deflected the blow.

"Never," he bellowed. He'd rather die than yield to this witch again.

Her boot slammed into his loins.

"Oomph." The air rushed from his lungs. He fell to his knees in the grass, clutching his hand protectively over the pained area as the haze cleared.

Rúna stood in front of him, panting, holding her sword at the ready with a mixture of shock and concern on her sweaty face. Her hand shook as she spoke, her sword wobbling back and forth in front of his face. "You are a sore loser, Wolf."

"Rúna?" He shook his head as the bloodlust seeped away, only to be replaced with horror.

What had he done?

She had drawn blood and he had lost all reason at the bitter reminder of his captivity. He'd attacked her, thinking she was the witch.

His heart sank. "I could have killed you."

"Not likely," she quipped, and sheathed her blade.

She could fight. Only a warrior could have matched him in the throes of bloodlust.

"You wield with both hands?" He shook his head at the extent of her trickery. Her breathlessness and clumsy moves of earlier had been a ruse. She had lulled him into overconfidence and bested him. His cock throbbed, causing him to wince once more. By Óðinn, she was beautiful, strong, *and* clever.

"You didn't truly believe that I couldn't fight, did you?" she mocked him.

He was a fool. She could fight as well as any of her warriors, mayhap even better, considering she could wield a sword in both hands.

Rúna smirked at his befuddled state, and then turned on her heel and strutted away.

His heart sank. He'd underestimated the change in her and the depths of her contempt toward him. He'd let his feelings for the Rúna from his past cloud him from seeing the woman she was now, a fearsome warrior, a woman that would fight to her dying breath rather than surrender. Admiration filled him at this new side of her. She would be a strong Jarl and a fierce mother who would raise strong sons. It only made him want her more.

Rúna flicked her braids over her shoulder as she turned to look back at him. Her eyes were as dark as a midwinter night, and just as cold.

"I'll never cede to a man again."

The hidden meaning of her words hit him hard in the center of his chest. She'd given him her heart and he'd broken it. She'd never forgive him, *ever*.

~

Under the dim light of the crescent moon, Jorvan held the flaming torch high and walked the boundary of Luleavst. It was a relief to escape the confines of the barn and the snoring of his men, though it did little to quell the edgy tension that possessed him. Not even a tortured slumber would come again this eve. The dream that had woken him in a shivering cold sweat was worse than usual, his mind replaying the long painful death of his child-hood friend, Elov, which he'd not even witnessed. As usual, thoughts of Elov left behind a hollow ache in his chest. He longed to feel his friend's back against his as they cut down their enemies. Would the pain ever ease?

Go back and mend it. He could still hear Elov's weakened voice echo across the cell they'd shared deep in the dark maze of caves.

You were always the strongest. You need to survive for all of us, Jorvan.

Curse the cruel gods—the blood of so many good men stained his hands. Men who screamed for mercy as the seiðkonur blade had cut their flesh night after night, until she ended their torment and offered them as a blót sacrifice. Men whose thick red blood had flowed across the stone altar in a ritual that called on the darkest of magic.

It is my fault that we are enslaved and so many have perished.

One by one, he had watched his men waste away and die from their festering wounds and fevers, until he and Elov were the only ones left. Each loss had stolen another piece of his heart, letting the darkness seep further inside him. At the end, Elov had fevered for weeks, and though neither spoke the words, they both had known he was not much longer for this world.

Coming here was a mistake, but it was not yours alone. You must return and tell our families of our fate.

They will never let me go.

Elov was adamant. *You must escape. They will take me out first this eve. I will give you the distraction you need.*

Nei. He could not allow Elov to sacrifice himself so he could flee like a coward.

But Elov had ignored his protest. *Find my father. He needs to know what happened, as do all the families.*

I'll not leave you. We can escape together.

Nei. I am too weakened. You stayed when you could have escaped. You were honorable until the end. Promise me that you will return to Rúna and live a good life together.

Later that night, Jorvan had stood over the freshly dug grave with his face upturned to the full moon overhead. Even in his weakened state, Elov had fought bravely, dispatching three of their captors before he was carried to the mighty halls of Valhalla to feast. He had buried his comrade with a boat, sword, and all the gold he could find in the small village. As he stood over the grave, still covered in the blood of the witch and the men who had defended her, his final words to Elov echoed in the deafening silence: *I swear it, Elov. I will keep my vow.* Then he had marched, as though propelled by the force of his friend's will, toward the noisy crescendo of waves crashing on the nearby coast.

Home. He'd heard Elov's whisper on the wind. *Go home.*

Jorvan held the flaming torch aloft, enjoying the cool brush of the night air against his skin. All was quiet in Luleavst, even the dogs that barked at the soft patter of the cats hunting in the dark. He stilled as soft footsteps approached.

"Brother." Valen emerged from the darkness, striding toward him with the easy confidence of a man whose ascension to Jarl was assured.

"Valen." Jorvan nodded at his brother and continued walking.

Valen fell into step beside him, his long stride easily keeping the quick pace.

Jorvan scanned the shadows, his silence showing his displeasure at the interruption. His oldest sibling watched him closely these days. No doubt tasked by their mother with ensuring he was not alone after a nightmare.

As though sensing his desire for quiet, Valen remained silent. In the years of his absence, Valen had become adept at tactful negotiation and noticing subtle signals, both skills that would serve him well when he took over from their father as Jarl of Gottland.

Jorvan could feel his jaw clenching, tighter and tighter, until a muscle near his chin ticked.

"You don't need to watch me."

He hated that his family knew the truth of his plight, but there had been no hiding it when he'd woken screaming and had to be subdued by his brothers until he came back to his senses.

"You were gone so long…" The heaviness of his brother's unspoken words hung in the air between them. Valen had missed him, worried for him. "Now that you have returned I am glad for these night walks."

They passed by the barn and rounded the bend that led toward the fields.

"The dreams are no better?" Valen asked.

Jorvan shrugged. "They are no worse. I'd give much to sleep like that." He motioned at three warriors asleep in the dirt where they'd fallen after downing too much ale in celebration of Rúna's win. One was without pants, his bare ass glowing like a waxing moon, and even from a distance the snores of another echoed through the night.

Valen shook his head. "They sleep like the dead."

The guard warming his hands by the fire as he kept watch over the half-harvested fields shifted, casting dancing light and shadows across the earth.

Jorvan scanned left, then right. The watch fire was positioned too far back from the fields to provide the vista needed to secure the area. Should he warn Jarl Isaksson? Nei. The man would never listen. He was too stubborn to see beyond his loathing.

"You would sleep too if you drank as much," Valen mused.

Jorvan shook his head. Even if he could bear the taste of what he'd once proclaimed was the nectar of the gods, he would not addle his senses willingly.

"It was drugged ale that led to our capture. I'll never risk being caught unawares again."

Valen walked beside him silently, as though his presence could provide the comfort he could not put into words.

"That is understandable, yet Rúna caught you unawares this day."

"Já. It will not happen again."

"Halt, let's talk." Valen grabbed his forearm and pulled him to a stop.

Jorvan reluctantly faced his brother. "I do not want to talk," he said, though he knew Valen would not cease until he had said his piece.

"Not speaking of what happened to you is why you cannot sleep. This must stop, brother. You need to talk about it so you can move on. And you need to tell Rúna about it. She deserves to know."

His gut roiled at the mere mention of *it*. It was bad enough he'd had to live it. He would not put that burden on Rúna too. "Nei."

"Stop being a fool! Look at what happened today. You lost control. You are not ready to wed, brother."

Was he right?

Valen continued. "You need more time. You cannot take this darkness into a marriage. What happened in the fight with Rúna proved that you are a danger to her."

He shook his head. "I can control it." Valen was wrong. He would never hurt Rúna. *Would he?*

"Stop lying to yourself." Valen ran his hand through his hair, his frustration evident. "If she had been a lesser warrior, you would have killed her. Are you willing to risk her life?"

His objection died as doubt wore away his steely resolve. He didn't want to hurt Rúna, but he had tried to do just that this very day.

The acrid tang of bile rose in his throat. The thought of losing her again was like a blade to the chest, but to lose her by his own hand … He would never forgive himself.

Valen reached out and clasped his shoulder. "It is not fair

to go into a marriage so wounded. If you cannot give her up then she deserves to know the truth before the wedding."

Jorvan pushed his brother's hand off his shoulder. Beneath his tunic, his flesh burned as a reminder that the darkness had not just taken his mind hostage, but his body too.

"Think on it, brother…" Valen released a heavy sigh. "And try to get some rest." After casting him one final somber look, Valen spun on his heel and walked back toward the village.

Jorvan stood motionless, watching his brother walk away. Was Valen right? Should he withdraw from the contest and let her chose another?

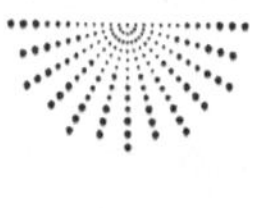

CHAPTER SIX

RÚNA

The next day, Rúna leaned against the weathered trunk of an old oak tree and studied the wolf as he watched her clansmen swimming in the cool waters of the river.

"It is unseasonably warm," Ásta said, as she wiped the water from her face with a towel. "I am glad that there is no contest this day, and that we can bathe before the long cold winter."

Rúna stretched her arms up over her head. "I am glad to rest a day."

Ásta looked at her with concern. "Do you still hurt?"

"A little," she lied. Her body ached from defending against the wolf's brutal attack yesterday.

Ásta glanced at where he stood alone on the riverbank. "His behavior yesterday was … unexpected … concerning."

"Já," Rúna agreed. "I have never seen him act without honor after a loss before." She had known something was wrong the instant that bloodlust had filled his eyes. She had seen it many times on the battlefield when men lost their wits.

Ásta wrapped the towel around her hair and squeezed the moisture from her long amber locks. "What do you think caused such a violent reaction? Did you say something to anger him?"

"Nei. I said naught. Something is not right with him." She knew it was the truth.

Even now, the wolf stood stiffly on the riverbank with his gaze fixed on the water rushing downstream, rather than swimming or relaxing with the other warriors.

"I have no doubt you will discover his secrets, Rúna."

"I will, and then I will use them against him."

Dànel was standing in the shade of an oak tree drinking ale and talking with Valen. To the casual observer he was deep in conversation, but she had been watching all of her suitors closely and all morning his gaze had kept returning to Ásta. The young man was lusting after her friend.

"Dànel wants to bed you, Ásta," she teased.

"Nei." A flush of rosy red crept across Ásta's cheeks.

"Já. His eyes follow you everywhere."

"I could not..."

"Why? There is naught wrong with taking what pleasure you can in this hard life. He is young, but gentle and kind." Ásta deserved happiness, even if it was merely fleeting moments of bliss found in the arms of a man. Not once in the four years since she had rescued Ásta from the battlefield where her husband had died, had her friend taken a man to her furs.

"I cannot." Ásta turned and hastened away.

"Give him a chance," Rúna called out, though she knew it would be ignored. Ásta's love for her beloved Njal meant she was unable to move on. She walked through life neither dead nor alive, caught in the gray abyss of grief and memories. It was difficult to watch her friend suffer so.

Rúna sighed and turned back to watch the wolf. She could do nothing for Ásta, but she could help herself. She needed to find a weakness she could exploit in the next challenge, something that would tip the scales in her favor.

He stretched his neck and looked up at the sky. His loose shirt flapped in the wind and fell open at the neck, the white fabric making his skin look as golden as the shimmering idols of Óðinn her father worshipped. He bent to pick up a rock, pausing to rub his fingers across it before skimming it out across the water. He ignored everything around him, not reacting to the joyful laughter of her clan nor the child crying for his mother. The tension in his stance told her he was alert, aware of everything, yet chose to remain alone.

Elin, the pretty swordsmith's daughter, walked out of the river toward him, swaying her hips seductively. The pale damp fabric of Elin's tunic did little to hide her breasts or hard nipples. She was a buxom woman and much favored by their clansmen, though none had succeeded in wooing her into marriage yet.

Rúna bristled at the overt display that signalled Elin's willingness to bed him. He would not resist her, men rarely did, and he had long had a taste for sampling women and discarding them. She'd been a fool to believe him when he'd told her none that came before meant anything after he had met her.

She huffed and watched him as he spoke with Elin. It was for the best that he find another and move on, for cert he wasn't getting anywhere near her furs. She should have sent a woman to him to distract him earlier. Mayhap if he liked Elin enough he would claim her and leave?

His jaw tightened and his long hair danced across his shoulders as he shook his head.

The smile fell from Elin's face, and it was clear that his rebuff had not been gentle when she stormed up the riverbank and onto the trail back to the village.

After her hasty exit, Leif Gustafsson sauntered over and offered a mug of ale.

The wolf shook his head and lifted the leather water flask that hung from his hip to his lips.

Rúna stilled. She had never seen him turn down cold ale. Had he truly changed?

He arched his head back, closed his eyes, and drank heartily.

Heat pooled between her legs. Freya help her, bathed in sunshine as he was, the man looked like a god.

Then a trickle of water escaped his lips, ran down his neck, and disappeared beneath his loose shirt.

The shiver that wracked her body shook her from the daze. She couldn't fall for his handsome pretence again, not when there was little of substance beneath. Mayhap he had changed some, but she doubted his reckless base nature differed. She was no lovesick young girl this time. She was a woman with a duty to her people, and she needed a man of honor and worth to help her lead clan Isaksson.

The wolf walked along the riverbank, away from the swimmers.

Rúna followed, edging through the trees silently, before leaping down onto the bank beside him.

He stiffened, his hand falling to the hilt of his sword, and then relaxing when he turned to face her.

She crossed her arms over her chest and ignored the shiver of pleasure that crept up her spine when his eyes dropped to where the fabric pulled tight across the swell of her breasts. "The women await you downstream."

He shrugged. "Let them wait. I want none but you."

She rolled her eyes. "Am I supposed to believe that pile of stinking horseshit? You want to be Jarl, like all the other suitors. Soon enough you would drink too much ale and fall between somebody's thighs. "

He shook his head. "Mayhap before, but no longer."

She scoffed and shook her head. "Before what?"

"It matters not. All I want is you."

She studied him. He was avoiding her question. "You abandoned me long ago, Wolf," she said, and feigned indifference, hoping that her eyes would not betray the truth.

"Calling me Wolf will not stop your feelings for me."

"I feel naught," she lied. Despite his betrayal, her body ached for him as much now as it had four years ago. Her heart thundered in her chest as the air between them thickened.

"Then say my name," he dared her.

"That man is dead to me, *Wolf*."

His eyebrow twitched, but he maintained his composure and cleared his throat. "Leaving you was a mistake," he said, his voice husky.

She swallowed hard, almost choking on her desire to believe him. She could feel the truth in his words and see the regret in his eyes. Her chest tightened, making it difficult to breathe. He did not get to do this to her, not again. How dare he come back here all regretful? He had no right, not after what he had done.

"And what of my clansmen, Wolf? Did you abandon them too?"

His body tensed as he recoiled at her accusation.

She smiled triumphantly. At last, a crack in that shield of

restraint and control that he wore like a warrior going into battle.

"Nei. They died, every single one of them."

"And yet *you* live. Did you even fight for them?"

He spat a curse at her and glared. "You speak of things you know nothing about, Rúna."

She ignored the fact that he'd reprimanded her like a disobedient child. She'd found a weakness she could exploit. She paused for a moment, taking in the rage that lit his gaze. Clearly the fate of his men disturbed him. Should she attack until he retreated? Já. She needed him gone—she would show no mercy.

"Tell me then, how did my clansmen die?"

The light in his eyes dimmed and he looked through her, out over the flowing waters of the river and off into the distance.

"Was there a battle?"

"The trials of battle were for babes compared to what we faced," he replied.

"The raid then—"

"There was no raid," he interrupted.

No battle. No raid. It made no sense. What else could have befallen them and caused so many deaths? "What happened to you?"

"We went ashore to get water and supplies so we could continue our journey. We came across a small village that agreed to give us shelter for the night and sell us supplies. That night we feasted on fresh meat and mulled wine. We were ravenous after so long at sea." He shook his head and sighed before continuing. "None of us realized that the wine was drugged. We woke the next morning as captives."

"You were a thrall?" She struggled to keep her cold pretence. Her father's thralls were treated kindly, but she knew it was not so elsewhere. "Were you captive all those years?"

"Já." His voice was a shaky whisper.

"And my men?"

He nodded, his eyes filled with despair. "They all succumbed to fevers brought on by the bloodletting."

Bloodletting?

A soft gasp escaped her. "Nei." She stumbled back, shocked at the thought of so many brought down in the summoning of favour with the gods. Bloodletting was a ritual reserved for the temple at Uppsala every ninth spring. Who would dare violate their laws so?

"Who did this?"

"A small clan ruled by a seer. They had lost many warriors and needed children. The seer used the blood to call on the gods to provide male babes."

She felt the blood drain from her face. That was not the earthly magic of the seers that surrendered to the will of the gods—it was the evil dark magic of madness and desperation.

His eyes were shadowed by guilt. "Your kin fought to the end, but there was naught I could do. I could not save them."

Rúna swallowed the lump in her throat. Her heart bled for all of those men who had not died the honorable death that would gain them entry to Valhalla. Her hand fell to her sword, her fingers flexing over the hilt with deadly intent.

"I will see the earth stained with blood for the suffering of those lost."

Laughter drifted on the breeze, the joyful sound doing naught to quell her dark thoughts of vengeance.

"It is done. I killed the seer."

The pain in his voice hit her like a blade to the chest,

sinking deep into her heart where it took root and reawakened the long-severed connection between them.

"You avenged them." She whispered the words, ashamed at the undeserved accusations she had thrown at him earlier. In that moment, filled with gratitude that he had honored her clansmen, she recognized the boy she'd once loved, now a man, yet just as willing to bare himself for her. He had changed—one could not endure such horrors and remain unaffected.

He pinned her with an agonized stare. "I did." His voice cracked as though the weight of speaking was unbearable, and then his mouth slammed shut.

She knew he would speak no more. Gone was the talkative boy of his youth—this wolf was a stranger. A stranger that she begrudgingly admitted had the heart of a warrior to overcome such horror.

"I am sorry that you and your men suffered, but it changes naught." His dreadful revelations had weakened her anger, and when he spoke of avenging the dead, she'd felt his unguarded anguish, but she could not let sympathy weaken her stance against him. She hardened her heart and continued. "I'll not give you pity."

He reared back, his shock evident on his handsome features. "I do not want it."

"Good." She was grateful he had told her the fate of her clansmen, but she could not wed a man she did not trust.

He looked down at her with undisguised longing, and his voice was husky as he spoke. "I want you."

Her stomach somersaulted at his declaration, but she shook her head. "At least you did not lose all honor," she said, then buried the yearning in her heart beneath the layered scars of his betrayal and walked away.

CHAPTER SEVEN

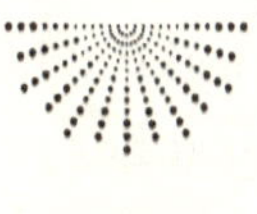

RÚNA

As the sun descended over the mountains late the next afternoon, Rúna curled her toes into the damp sand. Yet again, the wolf was her opponent in the final contest to win the second challenge. The wolf had proven he was more than just a capable warrior when he had outwitted the other suitors in the Hnefatafl board game tournament to match her scores. He was smart and strong—winning would require a new strategy.

She looked to where he stood, farther along the beach surrounded by his brother's warriors. As his dark blue eyes fixed on her, she knew she was entering dangerous territory.

His long hair flowing over his shoulders took her breath away. He looked every bit like the conquering Viking warrior as he walked toward her. She shivered and turned away. She couldn't let him get to her.

"Rúna, Jorvan." Her father pointed to the small boat bobbing in the calm waters of the bay. "The second challenge is a race to collect a ribbon from that ship and tie it around an apple tree in the garden."

She cursed under her breath. She was a good swimmer, but the wolf would be faster and he could outrun her with ease. She'd need to beat him back to the beach to have any hope of besting him. She stripped down to her undergarments and walked down to the water, contemplating her options.

"Rúna." The wolf stopped beside her and his eyes drifted down over the hardened peaks of her nipples beneath her undershirt, then looked up at her knowingly.

"Never." She hissed and shoved him in the shoulder.

He barely wavered.

Her eyes fell on the thatch of hair and thick staff hanging between his legs. By the gods, he was larger than she remembered. Why was he without pants but still wearing the shirt that would hamper his strokes?

"It is all yours, firefly."

She tore her gaze from his manhood and rolled her eyes. "Do not insult me by pretending you are here for anything more than my Jarldom."

"Your anger is justified, Rúna. It was wrong to leave you as I did, but I do not want your Jarldom. I want you."

Blasted man! Nothing she said riled him anymore.

Her father walked over. "Victory to the best Viking," he said, as the long mournful drone of the horn floated on the dusk breeze, signalling the start of the race.

The crowd jostled and shouted encouragement as they ran into the shallows, eager to see who reached the boat first before retreating to the orchard as the Jarl had ordered.

Rúna dove beneath the surface. She kicked hard and focused on slow steady breathing. She would best him. She had to.

His clean smooth strokes soon cut through the water beside her.

For a while, she matched his pace, but then she began to tire and he pulled away. She had to do something, now. She glanced up at the small bobbing boat. She couldn't let him get there first. She had to slow him down. She had to win—she could not marry him. She would do *anything* to avoid that fate. She reached out, grabbed his right ankle, and yanked on it.

His strokes faltered, and he paused to look back at her.

Now was her chance. She powered forward, pushing her arms and legs until they burned from the exertion. She was almost there. She could see Ásta leaning over the side of the boat with the ribbons dangling from her outstretched hand. Just a bit farther.

His body glided alongside hers as she reached the boat.

She grabbed the edge of the small wooden skiff and gasped for air as his hand settled beside hers. *Nei.* If he passed her, it was all over. She needed a distraction, something that would unsettle him and give her an advantage. It was time for a sneak attack.

"That was unfair," he said, barely panting as he looked down at her with mirth lighting his eyes.

"You naked is not fair." She reached out and grabbed him between the legs, fondling the length of his manhood. "This is impossible to ignore."

He stilled as she stroked his hardening length, and then his eyes drifted closed as he surrendered to her touch.

Her heart raced as she held his manhood in her hand, remembering the heady rush that came with giving him pleasure.

"Já." His voice was the low rumble of a man caught in the throes of satisfaction.

She stroked faster, and glanced up to where Ásta's shocked face peered down at her over the edge of the small boat. Undoubtedly, her friend would taunt her endlessly about this later.

She slid her thumb over his smooth bell shaped tip, then slowly reached up with her other hand and grabbed both of the ribbons from Ásta's hand.

"Rúna," Jorvan moaned, oblivious to their audience.

Now was her chance. She curled her feet up under her until they rested against the submerged hull, then released him and pushed off. She threw herself into the swim, pushing her body like never before. Her heart thundered in her chest as she swam as fast as she could back toward the shore.

"RÚNA," he bellowed, as he discovered that she'd stolen both of the ribbons.

She laughed, almost choking on a mouthful of water. It was less than what he deserved. She swam until her lungs burned and her arms ached, then staggered onto the beach on shaky legs. She looked down at the ribbons in her left hand, then turned back to look for him.

His body cut through the water with ease, barely hampered by the billowing fabric of his shirt.

Her heart leapt. He was nowhere near the shore yet. She grinned and stumbled across the beach to the well-worn path that led up to the settlement.

"Run, Rúna!" shouted the crowd gathered on the grass beneath the gnarled branches of the apple trees.

Their cries of support lifted her spirits. Her legs were heavy with fatigue, but she kept moving forward, buoyed by the knowledge that she would soon claim the victory that would allow her to choose her husband. Then she could banish the wolf, and the unwanted feelings his presence brought up in her, from her life. She was nearly there.

The shouts of the crowd swelled to a deafening roar.

A gust of air swished against the back of her neck. Her hand jerked as a ribbon slipped from her grasp.

"My thanks, firefly," the wolf yelled, his long legs pumping hard as he ran past her so fast that it felt like she was standing still.

She stumbled to a stop and watched as he tied his ribbon around the largest apple tree. Her heart dropped. He had won the second challenge and now they were tied.

"Jorvan, Jorvan," the crowd cheered as they surrounded him.

Rúna veered off the path and away from the crowded orchard. She would not let anyone see her distress. She avoided the great hall and made her way to the spring-fed bath nestled into the side of a grassy knoll for privacy, glad that she'd had the forethought to send Ásta to leave a dress there for her earlier.

Lush grass curled between her toes as she fumbled with numb fingers to remove her wet clothes and drop them beside the steaming circular stone bath fed by hot and cold springs from the nearby the mountainside.

She cursed the wolf under her breath and rubbed her hands together. He had snatched victory from her. She loathed being bested by him and was relieved that she was alone and could lick her wounds in peace.

A cool breeze wafted across her back, making her teeth chatter and forcing her to action. She pulled the leather tie from her hair and loosened her braids with shaky fingers as the sun disappeared behind the mountain, leaving behind the murky glow of twilight.

She stepped down onto the submerged stone ledge. A relieved groan fell from her parched lips as the steaming water warmed from her toes to her knees. She plunged into the deeper water, eager to wash the salt from her hair and chill from her bones. If only she could wash him from her life as easily.

"Well fought, Rúna," a voice said as she resurfaced.

Wolf!

Her eyes flew open.

He stood naked and unashamed on the grass, his wet shirt lying beside a flaming torch that cast flickering light over his powerful body. His intense blue eyes caught and held hers.

Time ceased moving as he stepped down into the water, his sun-kissed skin glistening around the dozens of silvery scars that covered his chest. Her eyes dipped lower, to where his manhood stood upright against his ridges of his muscular stomach. Blessed Freya, the man was more tempting than ale on a hot summer's day.

"Water?" He lowered himself into the bathing pool with one hand outstretched, offering her his leather flask.

Rúna eyed him warily. She was parched, but she didn't trust herself to be close to him. Everything inside of her screamed to stay as far away as possible for fear that she would succumb and quench her thirst on this rugged Viking. She'd felt an overwhelming rush of desire as she'd held his manhood in her hand out in the sea. Despite how he'd abandoned her, her body still wanted him.

"You do not want it?"

She didn't trust herself but would not let him know he affected her. She swam to sit beside him on the stone ledge, her body taut with nerves though she feigned a causal stooped pose, and took the flask from his outstretched hand.

"I did not think you capable of such deception Rúna."

She shrugged indifference. "You underestimate me." She emptied the flask and then placed it on the grass behind her.

He moved off the ledge and out into the deep, and then disappeared below the surface.

She sighed in relief then relaxed back against the cool stone wall with her legs dangling over the edge of the ledge. She would stay a while and then take her leave.

A few moments later, he re-emerged with a whoosh that sent water spilling over the stone edges and onto the lawn. He tossed his head, flicking his long hair back and sending a shower of water raining down over her.

She huffed her displeasure as she wiped the water from her face.

His nostrils flared as his eyes followed the slide of a droplet down her neck and over the swell of her breasts.

Her nipples hardened under his hungry stare. He looked like he wanted to lick it from her skin. Her gaze fell and caught on the scars that marred his chest. He had been honest about the bloodletting at least. Now she understood why he'd swum in his shirt. He would not want to explain his scars to the curious, nor be the subject of the rampant gossip they would incite.

His broad shoulders cut through the steam atop the water as he glided closer, giving him the look of a man blessed with an otherworldly magic.

"You could not best me without cheating?" he said.

She bristled at the insult, then sat up straight and leaned forward. "I. Did. Not. Cheat. I did what I must, to get what I want."

He closed the distance between them, placed his hands on either side of her on the ledge, and leaned in.

This close she could see the darker flecks of blue in his left eye and the tantalizing mole below his lower lip. She fought back the urge to pull him closer and press her mouth to his.

"And what do you want?" His low husky voice made the hairs on her neck stand on end.

A delicious warmth filled her, like warm pine-needle tea on a cold day, until she felt as though she would burst into flames. Blessed Freya, his mere voice set her body alight.

His lips curved into a satisfied smile.

Curse him! She was not a naive girl anymore. He would not use her desire as a weapon against her again. She looked down her nose at him defiantly.

"I want to kiss you," he whispered.

Her womanhood pulsed in response, and she realized that she wanted that too.

When she did not object, he slid a hand up the back of her neck, holding her firmly in place as his mouth covered hers in a tantalizingly slow and savoring kiss.

A shiver crept up her spine and she whimpered against his mouth. It felt so good. She needed more, much more. She wrapped her arms around his neck and pulled him closer, her pulse quickening as her nipples brushed against his hard chest.

As though he'd heard her silent plea, he twisted his fingers into her hair and thrust his tongue into her mouth in quick angry strokes that allowed no escape.

A delicious shudder heated her body as he wrapped his arms around her. She gasped in delight as his teeth sunk into her fleshy bottom lip and the sharp stinging pain drove her over the edge. She gripped his shoulders and met him with equal fervor in the frantic battle to control the kiss. Her legs wrapped around his waist and pulled him closer, until the hard ridges of his staff pressed against her soft folds. Freya, her body was on fire.

He rocked against her, his sex rubbing against the center of her pleasure, as his lips gentled once more into a soft kiss of lovers.

She was captive to the sensual dance of his hips, awash in

a sea of sensation and emotion that drove her steadily toward release.

His mouth left hers and burned a fiery path down toward her breasts. "Firefly," he whispered reverently.

She froze—the icy truth creeping back in to quell the fire flowing through her veins. *She couldn't do this.*

"Nei." She pushed at his shoulders, and then pushed again.

He pulled away and rose up in front of her. His eyes were still clouded by desire, and he was so close she could taste the sweetness of his breath on the air.

"What is it?" he asked.

"I want you to go. Leave Luleavst." She kept her eyes on the darkness over his shoulder, certain that if she looked at him she would surrender once more.

He cupped her chin in his hand, tilted her head back until she met his intense gaze, and studied her intently. "I am not leaving you again, Firefly. I love you."

He loved her?

Her breath hitched at his declaration. She could no longer deny that she still wanted to love and be loved, but not by a man that could walk away so heartlessly.

"You left once, you will do it again."

He pulled himself onto the ledge beside her and crossed his arms. He looked down at her, his hard, determined gaze leaving no doubt that he intended to prove her wrong.

Rúna swallowed hard. She couldn't lose herself in this man. She wouldn't survive the inevitable heartbreak of losing him again. But if he stayed …

Her pulse beat erratically.

… and fought to win her back, then eventually she would have to face the depths of her feelings for him. The very thought was terrifying.

"I cannot do this." She rose to her feet, hastily wrapped her towel around her body, and grabbed her clothes.

"Rúna, please stay."

She paused, barely resisting the urge to turn around. "Do not ask me to do what you could not," she said, then blinked away her tears and walked away.

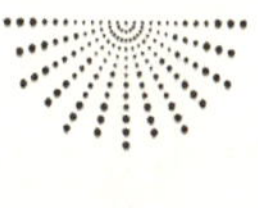

CHAPTER EIGHT

JORVAN

Jorvan paused on his patrol through the outskirts of the slumbering village to scan the shadows.

He couldn't sleep on the best of nights, and yet again, he'd woken thrashing and sweating with his legs wrapped up in the twisted blanket, to the drunken snores of his men reverberating around the barn. He had risen to walk through the darkness he loathed, intent on banishing his fear with each step of the boundary he traversed.

His mind wandered back to that moment in the sea when he'd discovered that Rúna's touch did not repulse him or remind him of the seer rubbing the oils into his skin. Rúna fingers gliding over his flesh had made him ache for her hands all over his body, and given him hope that maybe he was not broken after all.

And that kiss ...

Remembering the taste of her lips left him hard as rock and unsatisfied, so he walked, he walked, and he walked.

The soft scuff of a stone skidding across dirt broke the silence.

Something was wrong. He froze in the shadow of a large oak tree, icy tendrils brushing across the base of his spine and creeping slowly upward.

He squinted, peering into the inky blackness and wishing that a full moon replaced the crescent that hung overhead.

The faint tap of footsteps sounded out near the edge of the field where the golden barley was ready for harvest.

His hand fell to his sword. *Someone was coming.*

A crouched figure skirted along the edge of the field, crept behind the guard standing watch by the fire, and moved stealthily toward the settlement.

Were they under attack? Nei, not by an army of one. Mayhap this was one of Loki's tricks.

He followed quietly, cursing himself for not mentioning the weakness near the fields to the Jarl. Someone could have entered unnoticed. Whatever this intruder's intent, no doubt there was mischief or treachery afoot.

He studied the figure weaving through the outlying cottages taking care to remain hidden in the shadows cast by the trees and buildings. Whoever it was, they moved as though they were familiar with the village and accustomed to sneaking around. How many times had they done this before?

The intruder paused outside the Jarl's longhouse and looked left then right.

Jorvan caught a glimpse of hard eyes and a strong jaw before he ducked into the shadows cast by an apple tree.

The person approached the solid timer longhouse and glanced around furtively.

By the gods, they meant to enter the Jarl's home! He could not let the man, for he was now sure it was a man, get inside to where Rúna slept. He launched himself onto the intruder's back, shoving him forward and slamming his head in the large oak doors with a loud thud.

The man crumpled and fell to the ground unconscious. He would not be hurting Rúna or anybody else this eve.

Jorvan bent to check that the man still breathed, and then hurled the limp body up over his shoulder.

Muffled shouts and scuffling sounded from behind the longhouse doors.

He backed away, straining under the weight of his load as the doors opened.

Jarl Isaksson stepped outside, his nightshirt billowing around his bare legs as he roared. "Who is there?"

Bleary-eyed warriors holding torches and clutching their blades followed their Jarl outside as others emerged from the surrounding buildings. Rúna stood behind her father in a dark green nightdress and bare feet, the blade in her hand shimmering in the torchlight. She looked like a vengeful goddess.

"It is me, Jorvan." He stepped forward and tossed the intruder at the Jarl's feet, sending up a cloud of dust. "This man snuck past the guards near the fields."

When the Jarl raised his hand, signalling his warriors to lower their swords, women holding their children close flowed from the buildings to join their men.

Karl Isaksson crouched down and looked at the man's face. "Gunter Svensson, the dirty thief." He rose to his feet.

"He was banished last winter. He is the one that has been thieving this past moon," Rúna said.

Then Karl Isaksson stood upright and his eyes pierced the distance between them. He nodded once, a curt nod of acknowledgement shared between comrades. "My thanks, Jorvan."

Rúna's father spoke words of gratitude, to him, publicly!

Jorvan forced himself not to recoil in shock. He shrugged nonchalantly. "It was an easy capture."

The Jarl crossed his arms over his chest, his threatening stance a contrast to his respectful words. "Luleavst is in your debt, as am I. Your honor will not be forgotten."

Satisfaction filled him as he looked into the old warrior's eyes and saw respect reflected back at him. He recognized the hidden meaning in the Jarl's words and manner—their hostile past had been replaced with a warrior's respect. Jorvan nodded his agreement to the new accord between them and spoke his mind.

"Jarl, the guard's fire should be moved closer to the fields to offer a better view."

Jarl Isaksson turned to the warrior beside him. "Put Gunter in chains, and move the fire," he ordered. "Everyone else, back to your beds."

CHAPTER NINE

RÚNA

Rúna remained as the crowd of grumbling men and mothers shushing crying babies dispersed around her.

"What was that between Jorvan and your father?" Ásta asked, pulling her blanket tight around her shoulders. "Was there conflict with the Eriksson clan?"

Rúna shrugged and watched the lone wolf stride away holding a flaming torch aloft. The barn was in the opposite direction. Where was he going? The capture of the thief was surprising, but less so than the unspoken exchange that had occurred between the wolf and her father.

"I do not know, but it is clear that they have reached some sort of agreement." Now that she thought on it, Luleavst had not hosted an Eriksson since the wolf had abandoned her. Nowadays, her father sent their ships to Gottland to trade with Ràsmus Eriksson. Mayhap there was discord. Why would her father hide that from her?

She glanced at Ásta. "I want answers. I am going after him."

"It is cold. Take this," Ásta said, and wrapped the soft woollen blanket around her friend's shoulders.

Rúna hurried in the direction he had disappeared, until she spotted his hulking silhouette heading for the beach. Her feet were cold—she should have gone back for her boots—but it was too late now. She followed quietly, watching him navigate the winding path with ease. He was clearly not inebriated, unlike her warriors, who would pay for their sluggish response come morning.

Her foot caught on a stone and sent it skittering.

He glanced over his shoulder, his hair glowing in the fire-light as he motioned her forward and then strode down to the water.

She approached and stood beside him silently, curling her toes into the cool sand as she gathered her thoughts. The warrior that patrolled at night, caught thieves, and showed surprising self-control had reminded her of why she'd fallen in love with him four years ago. He'd always shown compassion for the less fortunate and beneath his light-hearted nature was an earnest drive to protect. She'd loved those parts of him that he'd kept hidden from the world. What a revelation it had been to feel safe with a man other than her father in a world fraught with danger.

He bent and thrust the torch into the sand at his side, and then stood beside her once more. Though they did not touch, they were so close she could feel the heat of his side against her own.

Back then, she had never thought that he would be the man to wound her most. His betrayal had felt agonizing, but she was glad for the pain that had pushed her to claim her own power, to become a shield-maiden.

The waves lapped gently at the shore as the quiet stretched.

She stared out into the darkness. How easily they had fallen back into the habit of sharing comfortable silence. It had always been this way between them, a familiarity, a peace, a sense of knowing and sharing without words. She turned to find him watching her.

"My thanks for catching the thief."

He nodded once. "I would see you safe."

Rúna looked at him curiously. "What quarrel do you have with my father?"

His brow furrowed and he hesitated before answering. "We have no quarrel."

She pinned him with a doubtful stare. "Not after this night, but what of before?"

He ran his hand through his hair and sighed heavily. "If your father has not spoken of it, then it is not my place to say. Ask him."

She bristled at his deft evasion. Why couldn't he tell her? What was he hiding? "Why were you outside this eve?"

"I was walking." He frowned and looked back out over the calm sea. "I sleep little nowadays."

She latched onto the momentary break in his defences. "Why?"

He turned to face her, his features marred by such pain and sadness that her heart ached in response. Whatever kept him up at night, it was raw, ugly, and filled him with regret.

She reached for him, her body heating as she caressed the hard planes of his chest and waited for him to find the words.

"Their screams wake me," he said, his voice cracking under the weight of his raw admission. His heart raced beneath her hand as he continued. "I see their faces as the seer cut them and forced me to watch. I hear their final screams as she sent them to Hel."

"Nightmares?" She slid her hand up and squeezed his shoulder.

His shoulders sagged and he looked at his feet. "Já."

Strong was a warrior that could admit such a weakness aloud. She had seen too many warriors to early graves as they'd buckled under the strain of keeping their inner battles secret.

"I spend my nights wondering why I was spared."

Her gut clenched at the memory of the gaunt, skeletal bodies of those that had fallen victim to the sickness of the mind and forgone food and water until their bodies gave out. She did not want that to happen to him. She would not wish that on her worst enemy.

"I am glad you did not die. Ale does not help you sleep? Or herbs?" she asked gently.

He raised his head, and she caught a flash of his pain in his eyes before they shuttered. "I cannot bear the taste." He shook off her hand and stepped away, as though the distance could break the bond of truth between them.

"But—"

"It matters not," he interrupted, then shrugged, feigning indifference. "I sleep less than most and am still twice as strong."

She nodded in response. He hadn't told her everything, but she would not probe further, not yet.

"Já. Gunter Svensson will curse that strength when he wakes in chains," she replied and turned to face the rising sun.

The tension eased from his shoulders. "That he will."

The cool water lapped at her bare toes as they stood shoulder to shoulder and watched the first rays of light shimmer across the surface of the sea.

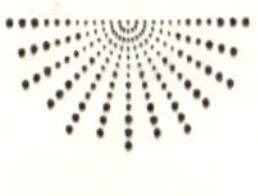

CHAPTER TEN

RÚNA

*L*ong after the meal had finished and mothers hustled children away to bed, Rúna drained her cup of wine and released a heavy sigh. She would soon have to make a decision and announce who had won her questions challenge. She looked at the young man at her side. Dànel Kvitfjell's gaze had followed Ásta around the room all night. She could not wed Dànel. She would not look the other way as her husband pined for another woman, and he was clearly besotted with Ásta.

She glanced around, seeking out the wolf.

He stood at the end of the table, leaning against the wall with his stormy eyes fixed on her over the brim of his cup.

She quickly doused the flush of heat that began to coil in her stomach and looked to the man she thought would make the most suitable husband.

Jàrri Karlsson threw his head back and laughed at a bawdy joke. He had a calm presence that put her at ease, and he'd told her that he wanted to settle down. The man was born to lead and determined make his way in the world.

The wolf's disapproving eyes stalked her every move. His fingers tightened around the same cup of ale he'd held in his hand all night. He had not drunk from it, not even when her warriors offered a toast in his honor for capturing the thief.

The scowl that hadn't left his face might scare others, but it made her want to crawl across the table toward him like a moth to a flame. Try as she might, she could not deny that her resolve was weakening under his steadfast determination to win her back.

She turned back to continue questioning Leif Gustafsson. "Your final question: how will you convince me to choose you?"

Leif swayed drunkenly as he pushed himself to his feet. He braced himself with one hand on the table and then slurred through the opening lines of a bawdy love poem.

Rúna stiffened. *How dare he?*

Hushed whispers spread along the tables like a wave filling the hall.

She slammed her dagger into the table and rose to her feet. Such words were the gravest insult to an unwed woman's reputation. She could not allow this slight to go unchallenged.

A hush fell over the room as all sensed the thickening tension in the air and instantly snapped to attention at the prospect of danger.

She poked her finger into his chest, wishing it were her blade. "Your words suggest intimacy that we do not share, Leif Gustafsson," she hissed.

His mouth curved into a mocking smile as he looked down at her and shrugged his shoulders. "No decent man will have you now. I am your only choice."

The urge to spill blood overwhelmed her. He knew naught of her if he thought that he could manipulate her by attacking her reputation. She would soon rectify his mistaken belief.

"You must fear losing to lie and cheat. Is the"—she looked up and down his massive body slowly, pausing on his groin before continuing—"little man afraid of being beaten by a woman?" Her hand fell to the hilt of her dagger, ready for him to retaliate, for she had insulted his honor and his manhood.

His face flushed red with unbridled rage.

She stood motionless and glared at him, itching for him to strike so she could challenge him to a holmgång.

"I fear none." He pounded a meaty fist on the table. "I would do *anything* to be Jarl," he roared, his treacherous eyes challenging her.

Hot breath caressed the back of her neck. She inhaled the scent of pine-needle soap and man.

"Jarl Isaksson has named Rúna his successor. *She* will be Jarl." The deep cadence of the wolf's voice sent a shiver up her spine.

She looked over her shoulder; he stood close, his body physically backing her as much as his words. The air between them heated, her skin burning like a wildfire where they almost touched.

"I am still Jarl, Leif Gustafsson," Jarl Isaksson roared. "You will leave my shores and never return. Remove him!"

She watched as three warriors rushed forward to do her father's bidding, struggling under the weight of the cursing and bucking man.

A cold brush of air hit her neck. She immediately missed the wolf's warmth as he moved back. Her stomach sank as she watched him walk away—it felt all too familiar.

Why was he leaving now?

Everything about him was confusing. He hadn't drawn

swords to solve the problem. He'd backed her, rather than try to protect her, and having him near left her breathless.

"Would you like more?" Ásta asked, motioning at the empty goblet on the table.

"No, thank you." Her mind was far from the festivities around her. Unlike the words that fell from his lips far too easily, the wolf's actions had convinced her that he wanted to make amends. She wanted to lay the past to rest too, but how did he expect to do that when he'd left yet again with neither an explanation nor apology? If given the chance, would he really stay in Luleavst with her, or would he discard her once more? There was much still unsaid between them, things that must be resolved, but even then, she was not sure if she could share his bed and let go of the hurt he'd caused her.

"I'll be back soon."

Trusting her powerful impulse to follow him, she exited the hall and ran after him. She needed answers.

"Wolf!"

He halted and held the flaming torch aloft, his wary stance softening when he recognized her. "What is it, Rúna?"

She stopped in front of him, noting his lack of expression. She'd have believed he was unaffected by her presence if not for his tensed jaw.

"Why did you leave?"

The scent of wood smoke wafted from his clothes, reminding her of that night long ago when he'd taken her innocence by the light of a campfire. She could still feel the grass between her fingers as she had clawed the earth and lost herself in the primal connection of earth, heat, and him. Nothing had prepared her for it to feel so pure, so right. In the years since, she had taken the occasional warrior to her bed and found satisfaction, yet nothing had ever compared to those nights with him.

He stared off into the darkness."I could no longer watch you with those fools."

Now that she was denied his gaze, she craved it. "They aren't here, yet you cannot look at me."

He met her needy stare.

Óðinn! His hooded eyes tore open the scar on her soul.

He is changed. He is changed. She repeated the words until her hands stopped shaking. She needed to know the truth of who he was now. It was time to look beyond the surface to the man beneath.

"You came uninvited to this gathering. If you wish for my favor, then you must answer my questions and finish the game."

"This is not a game." His intense gaze refused to release her. "I want you."

Her sex clenched at the wicked promise in his eyes.

"Ask your questions, Rúna."

She shivered at the sound of her name falling from his lips like smooth honey. "Why did you leave me behind that day?"

"I thought it best for you." He tugged on his earlobe and she knew he was lying.

"Do you expect me to believe that?"

"I was a stupid boy with little prospects. You were to become Jarl. You needed a man your equal."

"I thought you cared for me."

"I did. I do."

She shook her head at him in disgust. Only a fool would believe his lies. "Horseshit. You discarded me like soiled bathwater." She turned to leave, only to be halted by an iron grip on her wrist.

"Rúna…" He pulled her to him and wrapped an arm

around her waist. "I needed you to hate me so that you could move on with your life."

"Why?"

"So you would be happy. I knew that you would never give up on me, on us, unless you hated me. But if you hated me, then you would be free to love and be loved. I wanted that for you."

She leaned back, searching his face for the truth. It hurt to hear it, but his explanation made sense. She'd always known that something was not quite right about that day on the beach. She'd never understood how the man who had just a few hours before whispered of love and the future while he made love to her so tenderly, could change into the bitter hateful person that had embarrassed her so deliberately. She couldn't excuse his behavior, but now that she understood the motivation behind his hurtful words, they stung a little less.

"I am sorry that I hurt you," he said.

She did not want his feeble attempt at contrition. She pushed on his chest until he released her. "You apologize and now think yourself worthy? You will not find me so forgiving."

He flinched at her words, and then sighed heavily. "I do not deserve forgiveness, but I wanted you to know that losing you is my biggest regret. Even in my darkest days, thoughts of returning to you gave me the strength to keep on fighting so that I could return to right the wrong."

She raised an eyebrow. "Now you think yourself worthy?"

His face clouded with unease, but he held her gaze as he spoke. "Now, I am a man that will fight for what I want. It is for you to decide if I am worthy or not."

She looked at him doubtfully. Had everything she

believed to be true been a lie? "So you did not leave because you did not want me?"

He shook his head sadly. "Nei. I have always wanted you." He closed the distance between them and reached out to cup her cheek in his hand. His thumb skimmed across her bottom lip and his eyes darkened dangerously. "I always will."

Her heart raced at his confession. He wanted her, said he would fight for her. The warm glow that filled her was tempered by harsh pragmatism—the pull between them was strong, but she still had an unanswered question. Could she let their past go? She had to know. Would being in his arms always remind her of his betrayal? Or could she separate it from the man before her now? She could not go on without answers. If she couldn't do it, if she couldn't bear to have him touch her, then she must choose another. She must seduce him.

"How much do you want me, Wolf? Will you break the rules to have me?"

His nostrils flared. "Já," he growled.

Her gaze fell to his mouth. She ached to feel it on her once more. "Where would you take me?"

His lips crept into a wolfish grin and he near growled in response. "My ship."

A shiver raced up her spine. "Take me there."

The wooden dock creaked underfoot as they passed the carved dragon that stood guard at the bow and the painted battle shields that lined the sides of his ship.

She gathered her skirts and stepped onboard, then watched as he placed the torch in a sconce on a metal arm attached to the towering mast, and then turned to face her.

His gaze was at the same time tender and earnest as he advanced on her with long powerful strides.

Goodness, she was doing this. The thrill of anticipation

made her pulse beat erratically. "You'll not put the torch out? Someone might see us."

He paused mid-step. "The darkness reminds me of the caves."

"They kept you in the dark?" He'd not told her that before.

He nodded. "Inside a cave." He continued forward, his every step matching her one of backward retreat. "Worry not. I will hear if anyone approaches, though they will be feasting long into the night."

She knew it was true—none would bother them while the feasting continued. The back of her thighs hit the raised platform at the bow. Her heart fluttered wildly, but she resisted the urge to submit to the undeniably attractive power emanating from him. Instead, she straightened her shoulders and raised her chin. This time they would lie together as equals.

Three quick strides later he slid his thigh between hers, pressing the hard planes of his chest against her.

Óðinn, how she had missed his touch, his taste, his salty masculine scent.

He tucked wayward strands of her hair behind her ear and spoke in a low rumbling whisper that made her body quiver. "You would break your father's rules?"

"The rules matter not. When I win I shall choose my own husband." She ran her hands downward, over the shirt that covered his muscular chest.

"Who will you choose?"

Her breath hitched as his cheek caressed the side of her face, his beard creating a delicious friction that set her alight.

His teeth nipped at her earlobe, and then his tongue darted out to soothe the sharp pain. Her nipples hardened, sending pulsing messages to her sex.

She trailed her tongue across her dry lips. "I choose you … for now." She could barely get the words out for the lust consuming her, the flames fanned by the feel of his mouth moving across her jaw. She didn't know if she even cared about the pain of the past anymore. She believed that that man was gone. This man wanted to claim her, and she wanted to let him. All lingering doubt deserted her, replaced with an urgent longing to reunite with him in the sensual dance of mind and body that had haunted her sleepless nights.

She nipped at his lips, seeking entry.

A low rumble rose from his chest as his mouth opened to let her in, his response matching her hunger. He pulled her close and trailed his hands down the curve of her spine, the evidence of his desire firm against her stomach.

By the gods, he was large.

When his hands cupped her behind and lifted her against him, Rúna wrapped her legs around his waist and slid her arms up around his neck. He tasted of wild berries … and *man*.

"Delicious," she whispered.

Jorvan lowered her into the soft furs laid across the raised deck. He trailed a hand down her neck and stopped to lay it flat against the dip between her breasts.

"Are you sure, firefly?"

"I want this." She did not hesitate. Whatever the consequences, she had to know if she could lay with him. She wanted to take him into her body and lose herself in his arms.

She looked up, committing to memory the long curved neck of the carved dragon bathed in moonbeams as his hands tugged at her laces and he removed her dress and boots. She would never forget this night.

His heated gaze swept down over her naked curves, sending a wave of warmth to her core.

"Beautiful…" he murmured.

Her body arched as he took her nipple into his hot mouth and suckled hard. Shafts of need speared through her.

"More," she moaned and closed her eyes. Her hands clawed at his shirt, pulling it up over his head. She needed to feel the hard planes of his chest sliding across hers.

He rose to stand above her.

She looked up at his lithe form as he removed his breeches. Her eyes traced the lean lines of his muscular legs, her sex clenching at the sight of his thick cock sprouting from a thatch of blond hair to stand proud against the ridges of his stomach. She scanned upward, over the rise and fall of his broad chest, covered in fresh scars, to eyes that challenged her. His body, those eyes—her heart pounded in her chest like the beat of the hunting drum. Her body ached with an incontrollable earthy need to join with him.

"Come," she beckoned.

He obeyed, falling on her like a predator on prey, his mouth a cooling touch across her blazing skin as he sucked and bit a path across her neck to her breast.

She moaned as a flood of warmth flowed from where he sucked her nipple, down to where his fingers gently probed her tender flesh. Her hands stroked his chest. His skin was warm and soft except where her fingers brushed over the puckered scars. She kissed the worst one lightly, and then kissed his mouth long and deep as he settled between her legs, his hard length against her swollen flesh.

"Now, Jorvan," she demanded. If he made her wait any longer, she'd explode.

Ravenous need blazed in his eyes as he pressed slowly into her.

Her fingers curled into the soft furs and held on. *Blessed Freya!* It was perfect—he was perfect.

His hips thrust in a slow sensual dance that called to the wildness within her, his tongue teasing hers as she wrapped her hands around his biceps and matched his rocking thrusts.

"Harder," she begged.

He groaned in response to her need and increased his sweaty, savage strokes.

The fluid motion of his hips unlocked something within her, a belonging she thought she'd never find again. Delicious pleasure built until the first shuddering clench of her release spread through her body and her spirit soared.

Despite the passion so obvious in his movements, he gently wrapped his arms around her and dropped his head to the curve of her neck, before he made one final hard deep thrust and released his seed within her.

"Rú," he groaned.

Her heart cracked open as the endearment fell from his lips. He was the only one whom had ever called her that.

He shifted his weight from her, gathered her into his arms, and buried his face against her neck. "Gods, Rú. That was…"

"Já. It was…" There were no words, but they didn't need them. He'd felt it as much as her. She trailed her hands through his hair until his uneven breathing slowed and he slumbered against her.

~

*H*ours later, Rúna woke to the gentle rocking of the ship and a dazzling expanse of shimmering stars.

A lazy smile tugged at the corners of her mouth. What would dawn bring? She raised her hands above her head and arched her back, stretching to chase the stiffness from her limbs. The pleasure she had found in Jorvan's arms had left her with an undeniable hunger for more.

"Jorvan…" She rolled onto her side and froze as the blissful fog of satisfaction was torn away by a coldness that sucked the sated joy from her limbs. The furs beside her were now as empty and cold as the ice creeping back into her heart. He'd left her, again, just like the last time they'd made love and she'd awakened to find herself alone.

The tightness in her chest released as she realized that this time he'd left her because he could not sleep. Her heart ached for the distance that life's events had put between them and the people they had both become—her a warrior burdened by duty, and he a man so haunted by a dark past.

His honest confession had done much to heal the rift between them. Now when she thought about it, it was so obvious that he had lied on the beach that day. She should have known that the reckless smile intended to hurt her had really been a distraction to hide the pain simmering beneath his jerky movements.

"He was hurting too," she whispered aloud. Seda had been wise to suggest the trials—it had given her a chance to work through her issues with Jorvan and discover how she felt about him and the other suitors.

Years ago, she had been so caught up in her own suffering that she had failed to see the pain in his eyes as he had turned his back on her. The thought barely crossed her mind before another followed. Her fingernails dug into her palms as the truth hit her like a battleaxe.

"I still love him." She sat up, clutching the furs around her naked body. She had fallen in love with Jorvan, again.

What have I done?

A heaviness centered in her chest as she sat in lonely silence, the gentle salty breeze caressing her face. She had broken her vow never to be vulnerable to a man and love. She couldn't do this.

"A Jarl must never be weak," she whispered. So many times her father had said those words, but she had never understood, until now. It mattered not that her heart longed to wed Jorvan, she could not trust him. What if his brothers came and asked him to go raiding again? Would he change his mind and abandon her and the clan? A second betrayal would break her.

A pained whisper fell from her lips. "This was a mistake." She'd played a dangerous game and lost. She could not allow her own weakness to affect her duty to her clan. She needed a steadfast man to rule at her side.

I cannot risk it.

She should never have seduced Jorvan—now her body craved a man she could not have. She would always love him and cherish the memories of their time together, and after this night, she believed he would too. Letting him go would hurt them both, but she would soften the blow with a parting gift, a gift that would set him free to live a happy life without her.

A hot tear rolled down her cheek as she pulled on her dress and deerskin boots and then rose to her feet. She had to get away. Now, before he returned and she lost the will to resist him. She brushed the moisture from her face and fled, running along the wooden dock and into the safety of the darkness as though the hound from Hel nipped at her heels.

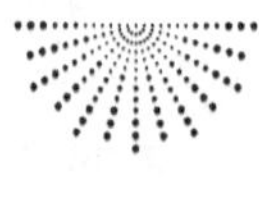

CHAPTER ELEVEN

Jorvan dipped his fingers into the foul concoction of moss, woollen fibres, and tar, and pressed it into the offending gaps in the hull of his ship. It was a fruitless endeavor, since the churning waves of the open seas always found a way through, but regular repairs like this were the difference between a manageable trickle and a sinking flood.

"Jorvan." Rúna stood on the beach, one hand shading her eyes as she waved at him.

He wiped his fingers on the rag and tossed it aside. He had not seen her since he'd left her in his furs to walk off his sleeplessness. By the gods, just the thought of her asleep in his furs had him hard again. He walked along the dock and across the sand to where she waited.

"We must talk," she said.

"I have to finish—"

"Now, Jorvan," she said, and turned on her heel.

He admired each flex of her toned backside as she strode along the shoreline toward the far end of the beach.

"Rúna?" He caught up as she weaved around some children wresting in the sand.

She shook her head. "Not here."

He followed her onto the trail that wound through the forest up to the cliffs where a guard watched over the bay. Eventually, she paused behind a large mossy boulder and turned to face him. "This…" She motioned between them. "It can never happen again."

"What are you saying?"

Her eyes betrayed her sorrow before she lowered her lashes.

He knew what was coming. She was going to push him away.

"You need to go home."

"Why would I leave when everything I want is in Luleavst?" He stepped forward, letting her see his hunger for her. If he had it his way, he would take her again here, now, against that boulder.

Her nipples hardened against her fabric tunic, but she shook her head. "You must."

He studied her closely, wondering what she really wanted. There was more to this jaunt through the woods than merely sending him away.

"I wanted to know…" She looked away.

A bird chirped overhead as he waited patiently for her to continue. Whatever she wanted must be important for her to seek him out like this, and he suspected that changing her mind about them being together would be dependent on his answer.

She straightened her shoulders and met his gaze with one of steadfast determination. "I need to know why you left. You owe me an explanation."

He hesitated. What had happened between him and her

father was resolved, but he couldn't lie to Rúna.

"I deserve to know," she demanded.

She was right. He couldn't expect her to trust him if he was not honest with her. He sighed and ran a hand through his hair. "When I left you that morning, two of the guards caught me sneaking back into the village and took me to your father."

She shrugged. "So?"

"I had a conversation with him that…" He stumbled over how to tell her without hurting her. "That made me realize I was not worthy of you."

Her eyebrows furrowed into a frown, and then she probed further. "What exactly did he say?"

He closed his eyes and swallowed hard before looking back at her. She was not going to let this go. "You have to remember that it wasn't the first time I had been caught."

She raised an eyebrow at him.

"Your father accused me of planning to overthrow him, of being a traitor."

"But you would never—"

"I know, but I had given him little to like of me, so he thought the worst. I told him that I loved you."

Her eyes widened. "You did?"

He almost choked on the words he knew would pain her. She adored her father and this revelation would likely cause a rift. "He said that if I truly loved you I would leave…"

As he spoke, the color drained from her face and she stumbled back against the boulder.

"… that a drunk like me would never be good enough for his daughter."

"So you left," she whispered.

He closed the distance between them and looked down at her. "Já. I left. Your father was right—I did not deserve you then. I would never have become a man if I had stayed."

She shook her head and loose tendrils of flaxen hair fluttered around her face. "How could he do that to me? He knew how I felt about you." Her voice cracked under the weight of her admission.

He gathered her into his arms. "He did it to protect you, because he loved you."

She shoved him away and rose to her feet, the vulnerableness of moments ago hidden once more beneath the stony-faced mask of a shield-maiden. "I have another question."

"Ask." He would tell her anything, give her everything.

"What happened to you when we fought?"

His stomach knotted at the memory of how he had lost control that day, how she could have been hurt. Valen was right. If he wanted her to be his wife then he had to tell her. She deserved to know that he was damaged, that being near him was dangerous.

"I … there is something broken in my mind."

"Was it the blood?"

He nodded, unable to look away, waiting to see disgust at his weakness cross her face. "It was the first time I had seen blood since my escape."

He saw no disgust or pity on her face. Instead, she looked at him thoughtfully. "It was bloodlust?"

"Já. When I looked at you, in my mind I saw the seer. I lost control."

"Is that why you freeze around Seda?"

He rubbed his beard. "You noticed that?"

She nodded back at him without speaking.

"Seda and the witch are one in my head. I am damaged, Rúna."

"Do not say such things." She shook her head and grabbed

his hand. "Come." She pulled him along the trail at a furious pace.

"I need to oversee the repairs to my ship."

"That can wait. I have a gift for you."

A gift?

He loved the feeling of her hand cradled within his as she led him through the forest, especially the hard calluses on her palms, born of years of weapons training, sliding across his. It had been so long since he'd been touched without feeling nauseous that he'd forgotten how good it felt. Now he never wanted to let go.

Finally, she stopped in a grove of ancient pines.

He looked up at the towering branches overhead, and then at the cottage on the other side of the glade. The small wooden house nestled against the mossy trunk of the largest tree had a fenced garden on one side and a small stream flowing alongside the other.

"Who lives here?"

The cottage door opened before Rúna answered, and a silver-haired woman stepped out.

He froze. *Seiðkonur!* His stomach lurched at the sight of the Isaksson seer.

Rúna squeezed his fingers. "It is time you met Seda."

He backed away, pulling his hand from hers. "I cannot."

"You can. You will. You must face your enemy to defeat your fear. I want you to be free, Jorvan. That is my gift to you."

Was Rúna right? He knew that he had no reason to fear the seer that had served her clan faithfully for decades, but the moment she was near all rational thought dissolved and he was plunged back into the darkness. Could facing Seda cure his fears? Or would it make everything worse?

"I could kill her."

Rúna's hand wrapped around the back of his neck and pulled his head down until their foreheads touched. "I'll not let that happen. I promise. You can do this."

He closed his eyes. If she believed it then he would too. He couldn't go on like this much longer. It was slowly killing him.

"She meddles too much for my liking, but she was right about the trials. You will see that she is kind." Rúna slid her hand in his and tugged him forward.

She is kind. She is kind.

"Well met, Seda. This is Jorvan."

His heart was hammering so hard in his ears that he could barely hear Rúna speak.

Seda smiled gently. "You may leave us now, Rúna."

He tightened his grip on Rúna's hand, desperate to make her understand that he wanted her to stay at his side.

"I'll not go far." She pried his fingers off and stepped back.

He followed her with his eyes, his panic increasing with her every step.

She stopped beside the stream and looked back to give him an encouraging nod.

He did not want to do this alone, he did not know if he had the strength, but he sucked in a fortifying breath and forced himself to look at Seda.

The seer's eyes were bright, not tinged with madness, and her gentle, calm demeanor chased away any illusions he had that she was a threat to him. The tension eased from his body and his breath came a little easier.

"There is darkness in you, Wolf." She swayed slightly as her eyes became glazed, and he knew she was communing with the gods. When they cleared a few moments later, she pinned him with a knowing stare. "You have been touched by a magic born of evil and fuelled by madness."

His stomach clenched and he fought the urge to back away as he felt the presence of magic in the air around them, rising and ebbing like a gentle wave lapping at the shore. This was not sinister or dark, it was a lighter earthly magic.

Seda tilted her head and studied him thoughtfully before she spoke. "You know that the balance was restored when you spilt her blood upon the earth."

He shook his head. If only that were truth. "Nei. She haunts me still."

The seer shook her head. "She has no magic hold on you, Wolf. When you release your fear you will be free."

"How?" He wanted that. Óðinn, how he wanted to banish the fear and be whole again.

She reached out, and slowly, as though approaching a skittish animal, placed her hand on his shoulder. "You will always carry darkness with you, but you need not fear it. The darkness is as much a part of life as light."

She speaks in riddles. What does that mean?

He flinched as she stepped forward and wrapped her arms around his shoulders.

"In time, you will learn to live with the darkness. Trust yourself, Wolf," she whispered in his ear.

Standing there in her embrace, Jorvan felt gentle warmth flowing through her into him. Tears pooled in his eyes. It was as if she was spreading a soothing balm over his scarred soul, and he knew, with absolute certainty, that there was no evil in her. His tormentor had hurt him because she was insane, not because she was seiðkonur. Instantly, his fear waned and he knew he would never fear a seiðkonur again. He tightened his arms around her for a few moments before releasing her and stepping back. Now, if he could just conquer the darkness within, he would truly be free.

"Farewell, Seda," Rúna called out as he walked toward her.

She took his hand in both of hers. "Are you well?" she asked, her face tense with worry.

He nodded and tucked stray hairs behind her right ear. "Já. I am glad that you brought me here."

She released a sigh of relief. "That is good, very good. I hope you go home less burdened than before."

He cupped her chin in his hand and smiled at her. "I am not leaving, Rúna. Never again."

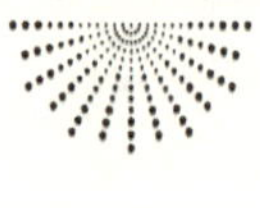

CHAPTER TWELVE

Two days later, Jorvan stood at edge of the woods with his wet clothes plastered to his skin and water running down his face. Dusk was nearing and the downpour showed no signs of relenting. Thor must be enraged to beget such a mighty storm. At least it would be easy to ensure Rúna victory in these conditions. She had to win. He knew with absolute certainty that anything his shield-maiden felt for him would turn to hate if she was forced into marriage. He would not let that happen.

"We wait no longer," Karl Isaksson said.

Jorvan looked around. The soggy field was deserted but for Rúna, Jàrri, himself, and the Jarl. Everyone else was staying dry inside, and Dànel had failed to arrive, likely distracted by the handmaiden he'd been wooing all week.

"Line up," the Jarl barked impatiently. He had been in a foul mood all day, storming around his longhouse, shouting orders and glowering at his warriors. Thank the gods that the Jarl had not discovered that he had bedded Rúna after the feast.

"You will not delay until the rain clears?" Rúna asked, looking up at the dark skies.

"Nei. I would see this matter resolved. A trail has been set with ribbons, follow it and find the rendering of the All Father. The first to return it to me will claim this challenge," her father replied, and then raised a curved goat horn to his lips and blew hard.

Jorvan leapt forward and sprinted onto the trail that cut through the thick forest, following the blue ribbons tied around the trunks of trees. He had claimed the lead, but he could hear Jàrri just a few steps behind him, and Rúna in the distance. He rounded a bend, his boots skidding in the mud as he grabbed a tree trunk to keep himself upright and slowed his pace. The trail was narrow and dangerous in these conditions and he could not afford to injure an ankle or leg.

Jàrri pulled alongside him as the trail widened, and then ran past.

Like Hel! Jorvan surged forward. He would let Rúna win, but he would not let another man steal his woman from him.

They had long left Rúna behind when the trail ended at a small meadow littered with the red leaves of the mountain ash trees that towered along the tree line.

He skidded to a stop beside Jàrri, struggling to pull air into his burning lungs. He knew much of the land around Luleavst, but none of this look familiar.

A murky stream cut through the meadow, its debris-filled waves crashing and churning with the same fury as the storm overhead.

He searched along the banks for the next marker. A chill swept up his spine. The stream flowed out of an opening in the side of the rocky cliff, and nearby stood a spear lodged in the earth with two blue ribbons tied below the iron tip.

Nei!

Not a cave. He couldn't do it. He couldn't face the damp darkness within, never again.

Jàrri looked at him and smirked. "Did you think her father would leave it to chance and let you win?"

Jorvan bristled. Was Rúna's father sabotaging his own contest? He had been so sure they had moved beyond past grievances.

"I overheard him saying that you were kept underground."

He clenched his teeth as Jàrri's words sank in. He may have won the Jarl's respect, but the man was determined to ensure his daughter remained beyond reach.

Jàrri pinned him with a determined stare. "Rúna is a remarkable woman. I want her as my wife and the mother of my children. When I win this race, Rúna's questions will be the final challenge, and she *will* choose me," he vowed, and then jogged across the soggy meadow and disappeared into the cave.

Jovan approached cautiously, his heartbeat increasing with every step. He knew what would happen if he lost control of himself—the dizziness, breathlessness, and crushing weight on his chest. But he had to do it, for Rúna.

He sucked in a fortifying breath and stepped inside, running his hand along the cool rock wall as he moved cautiously along a rocky ledge, testing each step.

The roar of water was deafening as it rushed by in the stream below, crashing against the rocks on its turbulent journey downstream.

With each step, he moved farther and farther from daylight into ominous black. He sucked the stale air into his lungs, never quite feeling like he got enough. This was madness. What was he doing?

A cool draft swished by as something flew overhead.

He crashed to his knees, and he was back *there*. Back in the damp cells, that smell of blood and decaying flesh, back listening to the terrified screams of his men. His heart pounded so fast it sounded like one long heartbeat in his ears. He leaned back against the cool rock wall and pulled his knees to his chest as he tried desperately to get more air. It wasn't enough—he couldn't breathe.

"Jorvan?" Rúna said.

He sensed her squat down beside him, and then her hand brushed the hair from his eyes.

"What is wrong?"

He groaned, unable to speak. He'd never wanted her to see him this way, ever.

"Is it the dark?"

He could feel the air in his lungs clawing at his throat, desperate to escape and let the fresh in, but his chest tightened even more. His own body was holding him captive.

"Breathe, Jorvan."

The gentle caress of her hand on his shoulder calmed him enough to exhale.

"Jàrri, something is wrong. He needs our help."

Rocks crunched beneath Jàrri's boot as he stepped around them. "He will survive. I have the Óðinn carving. Come with me, Rúna. I will wait for you outside and we can claim the victory together." Without waiting for her answer, Jàrri shuffled along the ledge back toward the cave entrance.

"Blasted man has no heart," Rúna cursed. "Breathe, Jorvan. I am here."

"Go, Rúna," he gasped out. "You must win."

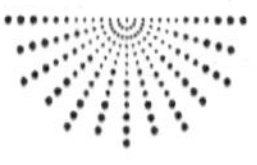

CHAPTER THIRTEEN

RÚNA

Rúna hesitated with her hand on Jorvan's shoulder. If she stayed to help him, then she would never catch Jàrri, but the water was rising fast, and if she left Jorvan when he was trapped within his own mind like this then he could drown.

His body shuddered as he released shaky breaths, and then his hands came up and he pushed her away. "Go, Rúna."

Nei. She would not abandon him, not when he needed her most. She gripped his head in her hands and pressed her forehead to his.

"I'll not leave you to die. We will get out of here together." She placed her hand in his and rose to her feet. "Come. The water is rising. We must go."

Jorvan steadied himself against the cave wall as she pulled him upright.

"You go first." As she stepped back to give him room to pass by, her foot slid across a moistened rock and she stumbled. Panic tore at her insides. She teetered for a moment on the edge, her arms flailing desperately as she fell backward.

The cold stole the breath from her lungs as she hit the water and was pulled under. She swam frantically upward until she burst through the surface.

"Rúna!" Jorvan's shout echoed like thunder in the cave.

She gulped down a lungful of air and searched the ledge above for Jorvan as the rushing water tossed her back and forth. Time slowed as she stared up into his terrified blue eyes. All would be well. He would pull her out.

Then he turned and ran away from her.

Her stomach dropped. He'd left her. Her heart shattered beyond repair.

He'd left her to die.

She looked around wildly, searching for something to cling to and hold herself above the raging water. Her nails scraped across the smooth rock walls and tore as she struggled to find purchase. Then the water pulled her under again, tearing at her from all sides and forcing the air from her lungs as it dragged her down to the bottom.

Her heart raced as the heavy water held her down, her fingers scraping across the mud as her lungs threatened to burst. Though she fought it, her mouth opened and she sucked in dirty, gritty floodwater that made her lungs burn. Then the darkness consumed her, and she felt herself slipping through the veil to the otherworld.

Images of her father, her clan, and Jorvan, flashed before her eyes. Moments in time, flashes of a life that was slipping away.

Nei.

Fury surged within her. She did not want to die, not yet, not when her people still needed her. The muddy bottom oozed beneath her toes as she kicked off with a renewed surge of hope. She would not die like this. She was a warrior —she would have an honorable death and feast in Valhalla.

She burst through the surface with a splash and strong fingers grasped one of her hands as her other one caught on a rock. She dug her fingers into the craggy surface and held on, coughing and gasping as she inhaled the damp air. Now that she could breathe and hold herself above the rushing water, she could see a small ledge downstream that she could climb onto and then make her way back up the rock wall. It was not far, but she would have to let go and swim.

"Rúna..."

She turned towards his voice.

Jorvan lay flat on the ledge, half of his body teetering over the edge with his arms outstretched. He squeezed her fingers. "Let go. I've got you."

"Nei." She couldn't do it. It would be better to risk the swim and rely on herself. "You left me." She focused on the ledge and prepared to kick off the rock.

"Nei, Rúna. My way is safer. If you try to swim you will die."

She shook her head, though doubt began to creep in. She needed to make a decision. Her arms burned with fatigue from struggling to stay on the rock. She could not hold on much longer. Should she let go and use the last of her strength to try and swim to the bank or trust him to catch her?

"Let go, firefly. Let's do it together. Trust me. I love you."

As she glanced up at him, lying dangerously off the edge and risking falling into the water himself, she could clearly see the anguish on his face at the prospect of losing her. The puckered scars on his chest flashed in her mind—this cave was his worst nightmare, yet he had faced it for her, for the chance to marry her. Walk into the darkness, face death, he would do it all for her.

Even now, his chest heaved as panic threatened to overwhelm him once more, but his hand remained outstretched. He stayed.

Realization washed over her. He would not fail her this time. She could trust him with her life. She shivered, looking at her fingers in his grasp. They were blue. Why were her eyelids so heavy? *So tired ...* She let her fingers slip from the rock and threw her hand up over her head as the current took her.

Strong fingers wrapped around her arm and Jorvan grunted as he dragged her up onto the ledge beside him.

She sagged against him as she struggled for breath, stiff with the cold. *She'd been right to trust him.*

"Gods, you scared me, Rúna." He swept her into his arms. "The flood is making the ledge crumble. We must go."

She wrapped an arm around his neck and held on as he carried her out into the storm and carefully lowered himself to the ground with her in his lap. His hands swept over her limbs, searching for injuries.

"You saved me," she said.

He grasped her face between his cold hands, his voice shaking as he spoke. "I will always protect you, firefly, always."

A lump formed in her throat. "I thought you were leaving me when I fell in the water and you ran away. I couldn't bear it." Her shoulders heaved, a sob breaking free as she gave voice to her greatest fear.

His arms tightened around her. "Look at me, Rúna."

She looked up at him through watery eyes.

"The ledge was too high where you fell in, so I ran downstream to find somewhere I could reach you as you went past." His blue eyes were lit with a fierce determination. "I love you, Rúna. I will never leave you again."

"Never?"

"Never. It was thoughts of coming home to you that sustained me in that dark cave. *You* were the reason I lived through that nightmare. If you had died in that water, I would have followed you."

Rúna sobbed, never for a moment doubting that he spoke the truth. He loved her. She pulled him down, her mouth covering his hungrily, her lips moving with the desperate reckless abandon of a woman that had cheated death.

He pulled back, his breath misting against her face. "In the darkness you were my light. You are my light…"

With his words, the last of the pain Rúna had used to shield her heart against him shattered and scattered on the blustering wind.

"Jorvan…" she whispered, and then moaned in approval as he claimed her mouth in another fierce kiss.

CHAPTER FOURTEEN

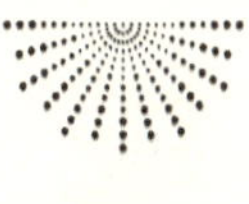

RÚNA

The next day, as the sun rose on the horizon, Rúna prepared for the wedding ritual. With herself, Jorvan, and Jàrri all claiming one win each, it would be her questions that would decide who would become her husband after all. Her father had not protested the outcome. Mayhap realizing he had almost lost her in that cave had made him see the foolishness of his contest? Whatever his reasons, it was a relief to be in control of her fate once more.

The mist that invaded the pine forest swirled around her ankles as she warmed her hands at the crackling fire. She curled her toes into the damp moss underfoot and inhaled the earthy air that left a sweet tang of the forest on her tongue.

Her mother and father stood off to her left, proud smiles on their faces as they watched the clan surround her in a wide circle, their bodies swaying with the slow drumming that echoed through the trees.

Rúna closed her eyes. She was exhausted from the long sleepless night spent pacing her room as she pondered her choice. She was thankful to be alive, and that Jorvan had saved her, but she wasn't the same girl as five years ago. Her life wasn't so simple anymore.

She watched the seiðkonur approach, one hand clutching her long carved staff. Her tall bony form was clad in a gown dyed the rich red tones of the lingonberry, and her silver hair, decorated with beads and feathers, fell in gentle waves to her waist.

"It is time," Seda said, and then blew a carved goat horn to call the men forth.

Rúna's chest tightened as the masked men entered the clearing. Her eyes flicked between the eagle and lynx, avoiding the wolf she knew followed her every move. As much as she tried, she could not keep her mind from returning to the moment she had first seen him in the wolf mask, before she had known it was her beloved Jorvan, and the wicked response of her body to the dangerous predator with those blue eyes.

Seda dipped a small twig brush in the cauldron beside the fire and flicked an offering of mead on the damp earth. "The gods foretold of a man of wit, brawn, and heart. Though the contest is tied, there is one that has shown heart." The seiðkonur looked pointedly at Jorvan, before turning her gaze on Rúna. "Yet, there is one final challenge to be decided. Rúna, do you have a final question?"

Rúna pushed away her doubts and firmed her resolve. "Have you loved before?" she asked, before she even realized the words fell from her mouth.

The eagle nodded, his eyes sad beneath the white crown of feathers. "Já. I love another."

"My thanks for your truth, Eagle." She turned to face the lynx.

"Nei," he said, smoke wafting around his tufted ears and

up towards the gods like an omen. "I have never loved." She'd suspected as much. Jàrri Karlsson was free from attachments.

She turned to meet the steely blue gaze of her beloved.

"I loved a woman once." Jorvan's voice was thick with emotion. "I was led astray by the promise of adventure and I let her slip away. It was a foolish mistake."

The eerie green ribbons of the northern lights danced across the sky above him.

"There is no adventure, no treasure, and no gift greater than a woman's love," he continued.

"They are pretty words, Wolf. How am I to know they are not empty?"

He strode toward her.

Her father stepped forward to intervene, but Rúna raised a hand to stay him. She'd hear Jorvan's answer and lay whatever was between them to rest forever.

"My heart belongs to her, my firefly."

Her heart skipped a beat at his words. Time slowed to a crawl. The world around her disappeared as their eyes locked and a new awareness flowed between them.

The seiðkonur cleared her throat.

Rúna rested a hand on her hip and looked down her nose at him. "Did you say pretty words to this woman you claim to love, and then sail away?"

"I'm no longer that boy. I would never leave her again."

The seiðkonur's lips curved into a knowing smile.

Rúna watched him, weighing his words. "You are back now. Why wait so long to claim her?"

"I returned to my father to ask him to negotiate for her hand and learned that she already planned to wed. I came as fast as I could."

A shocked murmur swept through the clan as they realized he spoke of Rúna.

"And if she is no longer that girl you knew?"

"Then, I will love her more for it."

"And if she chooses another?"

"I trust her. Whatever she chooses this day, my love and
life will always be hers. She is my heart."

Seda waved her arm and her apprentices began to beat
the ancestral drums once more. "Enough delay. Rúna,
daughter of Jarl Eriksson, give this cup to the man you
choose and you shall be wed."

Rúna took the cup of honey mead from the seiðkonur's
outstretched hands. It was time. Time to choose the life she
wanted. She couldn't marry another—her heart belonged to
him and she'd be foolish to deny it. The prophecy the seer
had foretold was truth. Her Viking warrior was a man of wit,
brawn, and heart. She was his she-wolf, and just like the
wolves, she'd mated for life.

She stepped forward.

Jorvan stiffened as she moved toward Jàrri Karlsson, his
hands balling into tight fists when she paused in front of the
man standing beside him.

She smiled and nodded at Jàrri. "You are a worthy opponent, Lynx. You have represented clan Karlsson with honor."

Then, she raised the cup and quickly sidestepped to offer
it to the man she'd always loved, letting her eyes reveal her
mischief. "I choose you, Jorvan."

He raised his hands, refusing to accept the cup. "I cannot
do it like this."

The colour drained from her vision and the world turned
gray.

He pulled the wolf mask from his face and tossed it aside.
"There will be no more secrets—or oceans—between us." His

cheek brushed hers as he bent and whispered in her ear. "You'll regret making me think you chose another, firefly."

She pressed her hand to his chest and stretched up onto her toes. "It was always you," she whispered.

To watching eyes, it appeared he didn't react, but she heard his sharp intake of breath.

She traced a fingertip along the faded scar that curved up his unmasked face. It was perfect on her beloved Viking warrior.

"Rú…" He twined his fingers with hers and tugged her against his chest.

She sipped the honey mead, and then pressed the cup into his hand. Every part of her knew that this was where she belonged, with him, and with her people.

"Drink."

He sipped the liquid she knew he loathed, and then slid a hand up into her hair and pressed his forehead to hers.

She curled her arms around his neck, her lips curving into a satisfied smile.

"You are mine now, Wolf."

AFTERWORD

Thank you so much for reading Rúna and Jorvan's story. I hope you had a wonderful time with them as they found their way back to each other. Authors love reviews. If you enjoyed this book, please consider leaving a review at your place of purchase.

Would you like to hear about my latest news and releases? You can sign up for my newsletter at www.reethornton.com

If you enjoyed Beloved Viking, you'll love the second Viking Hearts novella. Here's a sneak peak!

Forbidden Viking

An Arabian Princess tastes freedom...

When Samara Abbasid's ship is attacked she throws herself overboard and seeks refuge in the Viking Jarldom of Gottland. Claiming to be merely a scribe, she temporarily escapes her life of duty and expectation, and is free to sample the Vikings ways. She finds them as seductive as the strong Jarl, Valen. However, if Valen discovers her royal status he could use her as leverage in his trade negotiations with her father, the powerful Caliph. Worse, she must soon return to the royal court and her upcoming arranged marriage. But once she's tasted forbidden pleasure will she be able to return to a life of duty...?

A Jarl bound by duty...

The most powerful Viking clans are assembling on the isle of Gottland to celebrate Valen Eriksson's ascension to Jarl. So Valen is furious to discover rogue Vikings have raided in his territory. Now he must serve swift justice and protect the mysterious survivor until he can return her the Abbasid Caliph. The last thing he needs is to be tempted by the alluring scribe, not when he's sworn to choose a bride from an allied Viking clan. Duty to his clan has always been first and foremost, yet his heart yearns...